DIAMONDBACK McCALL: THE SWORD OF EL DIABLO

Other books by Robert Middleton:

Diamondback McCall: Island Lost
Diamondback McCall

DIAMONDBACK McCALL:
THE SWORD OF EL DIABLO

•

Robert Middleton

AVALON BOOKS
NEW YORK

Published by Thomas Bouregy & Co., Inc.
160 Madison Avenue, New York, NY 10016

Middleton, Robert, 1950–
    Diamondback McCall : the sword of El Diablo / Robert
Middleton.
        p. cm.
    ISBN 978-0-8034-7771-1 (acid-free paper)
    I. Title.
    PS3613.I3625D54 2010
    813'.6—dc22

                                        2010005248

PRINTED IN THE UNITED STATES OF AMERICA
ON ACID-FREE PAPER
BY HADDON CRAFTSMEN, BLOOMSBURG, PENNSYLVANIA

To my good friend, Rick Ciauri, who was so generous with his time and editorial talent, my sincere appreciation.

For their thoughtful comments and suggestions,
my thanks to the following special people:

Skip Middleton
Denise Middleton
Rita and Larry Bittner
Carol Biller

Chapter One

An Unfriendly Town

Smoke lingered over Tucson in the still morning air. Throughout the town, stoves had been lit in preparation for breakfast, and for warmth. Although the sun had been up a few hours, there was a brisk snap to the air. The long summer of 1884 had finally given way to a chill fall.

Jack "Diamondback" McCall and Dakota Dan Smith rode into Tucson as the town was just coming to life. They tied off their mounts in front of the bank and saw that it, like most of the city's businesses, was not yet open.

With around a half hour to wait, and Dan's usual inclination for vittles, they headed up the boardwalk toward a small cafe and bar.

After passing a half-dozen storefronts, a single rider approached from up the street. As he rode closer, Jack took notice of the young man. He had the cold, hard look of a gunman and the hardware to match. He also looked to be prosperous at it. Beneath his sienna leather jacket was a pressed white shirt. The rest of his duds were beige, and expensive. He wore his single Colt revolver below the hip, with the holster tied snugly to his right thigh.

The rider plainly had at least as much interest in Jack, and the two men exchanged stares. Of course, it wasn't unusual for Jack to draw attention. He was used to that and accepted that it simply came with his name and reputation. But clearly, this gunman had a special interest in him.

The rider continued on until he was at the point where he was adjacent to Jack and Dan, and pulled his horse up short. A thin smile briefly appeared on his young face. Then he immediately spun his sorrel colt around and spurred him smartly up the street. After putting a dozen or so buildings between himself and the two men on the boardwalk, he stopped, dismounted, and tied off his horse.

Jack and Dan looked to each other without speaking. They both shook their heads and continued on their way. The young gunman, as expected, stepped onto the boardwalk and turned their way. As they drew closer, the pace of all three men slowed, and with only a few steps between them, they stopped.

There were a few moments of silent face-off. The young gunhand seemed confident and slightly excited.

Jack looked at him with indifference, his handsome features showing no sign of concern. No one man had a chance against him. Jack sensed that he was being measured, or judged, and wondered if the young shooter knew who he was. The fact that Jack was a tall and tough-looking hombre wouldn't indicate that he was a man famous for his lightning draw. However, his attire might. His customary black riding clothes, replete with snake-skin trim, did tend to suggest just who and what he was. If that wasn't enough, a glance at his two pearl-handled Colts, with the initials JDM on the holsters, surely would. And that was where the gunhand's eyes were focused.

The shooter looked at Jack with a smirk of satisfaction, and gave a single nod. "Thought it was you." He added two more nods. "Mr. Diamondback McCall, himself! This must be my lucky day."

"I got a feelin' it's gonna be your last, sonny," Dan stated solemnly.

The young man had given Dan token notice, dismissing him as no threat. Of course Dakota Dan looked more chubby than tough. He was wearing his usual white shirt, tan suspenders, and denim pants. They showed nearly as much wear as his weathered round and bearded face. So did his old buckskin coat and crumpled off-white Stetson, which he wore way back atop his thinning gray hair. Dan wore a single Colt on his right hip, but he looked more friendly than dangerous.

The young gunman kept his cold eyes locked on Jack, while giving a tilt of the head toward Dan. "I don't usually shoot old men, but today I might make an exception. Tell your friend to move on, my business is with you."

Jack decided that in this case, it probably was best for Dan to go. Not because he was in any particular danger, but because he thought there was a better chance of getting the shooter to back down without an audience. "Maybe you ought to wait at the eatery, partner, I won't be long."

Disappointment was evident on Dan's face. He surely hated to miss the show. Nonetheless, he gave a nod and moved along, knowing that Jack wouldn't have asked without a good reason.

Once Dan was a few doors down, Jack took a step closer to the shooter—they were no more than a few feet apart. He looked calmly at the young man. "All right, son. What's your business with me?"

"They're offering a thousand pesos for you down in Mexico."

"Ah, that. So, you figure on collecting it?"

He gave a couple of nods and a confident expression. "The reward says 'dead or alive.'"

"But you've got to be alive to get that reward. You think you're good enough?"

The smirk reappeared on his face. "Ask anyone, they'll tell you. I'm the fastest gun in town."

"Maybe, but I don't live here."

Anger flushed the gunman's face. "If you're so fast, why'd you have to gun down two unarmed men in Nogales?"

"It didn't happen that way."

"There was a witness, McCall."

"Some men will lie if it suits their purpose."

"So, you're saying he just made it up?"

"That's what I'm saying, son."

The shooter's expression showed impatience and disbelief. "I know about you, McCall, doing trick shots in that show, and quick draws for the crowd." He shook his head. "But they're not shooting back. It's different when you're facing a fast gun!"

"You might be fast, but not fast enough."

"You've never seen me draw."

"Son, nobody's ever seen me draw," Jack stated matter-of-factly, and looked hard into his adversary's eyes. He could see that further words were useless, and the young gun was close to making his move. So, Jack decided not to wait. Without a change of expression, and in less than a blink of an eye, he drew both Colts. It happened so fast that the gunman didn't even have time to react. He had a look of astonishment, as though questioning his own eyes. For a few seconds Jack aimed the two pistols right at the gunhand's nose. In response, he simply stared down the barrels, momentarily frozen.

Jack allowed himself a slight smile before spinning his Colts, one at a time, back into their holsters. "I guess you weren't ready, son. So, why don't you go first this time." His smile grew a little. "Don't worry about me, I'll catch up."

It seemed as though all the confidence and pride had drained from his young face. His right hand wavered some beside his gun. Just a trace of tremor was noticeable in the fingers.

It wasn't Jack's nature to humble a man, unless he had it coming. In this case, it only seemed right that the cocky young shooter knew how it felt to be on the wrong side of a faster gun.

As the gunman stood frozen and fear seemed to engulf him, Jack stared hard at him. "So, you gonna draw down, or back down." The corners of his mouth curled up a bit. "You shouldn't let little things like common sense or fear stop you. After all, you're a shoo-in for second place."

The young gun just stood there, speechless, not appreciating the sarcasm.

"Let's get on with it, son. If I've got to kill you, I'd just as soon get it over with."

After a few more seconds of indecision on the young man's part, Jack finally took a step closer and put his left hand on the handle of his opponent's revolver. "All right then, son. I'm not gonna kill you, but I'm taking the gun." Jack gave him another cold stare while retrieving the shooter's pistol and then sliding it behind his own belt. "You come my way again and I won't be so generous!" With that last statement, he simply pushed the young gunman aside, and headed for the eatery.

As Jack walked along, he wondered, as he always did after showing mercy to a killer, if he'd later come to regret it. In this case he was willing to accept the risk. That young gunhand didn't strike him as a bushwhacker. He also left that shooter questioning everything he believed in himself. Jack knew it came down to a simple fact. A gunslinger without confidence had better start looking for another line of work.

Dan had been watching from the doorway of the small establishment called "Cafe Jose." He met Jack with a single shake of the head. "That young feller didn't seem any too friendly, partner." Dan then motioned toward a table in the far right corner of the restaurant-bar.

While they crossed the room, Jack said, "Seems like there's one of his kind in every town."

Once they settled in behind the table, Jack gave the place a brief scan. Tables filled the space between him and the bar, with a tiny kitchen on the other side of it. A cheerful Mexican manned the dark oak bar, while a very busy senora worked the pots, pans, and iron stove.

It seemed that the middle-aged couple were the owners, and business was good. Four cowpokes were standing before the bar. Three more men were sitting at a table in the corner to his right. One other man then passed through the doorway and took a chair at a table between them and Jack.

Since Dan had already placed their order, the barkeep was soon bringing a couple of cervezas. As he made his way back to the bar, Jack and Dan settled back in their chairs and took swigs of their beers. Dan noted a troubled expression on his partner's face, a look he'd not seen before. What's on your mind, Jack?" Dan took another sip.

Jack put down his mug and answered without quite looking his friend's way. "That gunslinger believed those men I killed in Nogales were unarmed."

"Well, we know who to thank for that. It only figures. When you killed Tex Foley, his brother swore revenge. Now he'll do anything to get even. And when he sent those two hired guns to kill you, and that didn't work, he lied to the Federales. Simple as that." Dan saw the same expression on Jack's face. "Those hired killers didn't give you any choice, Jack. Neither did Foley's brother."

Jack gave a shake of the head. "I've got to square myself with the Mexican authorities."

"You calculate there'll be others lookin' to collect that bounty on your head?"

"That's only part of it." He looked straight into Dan's eyes. "I've got to clear my name. I don't like being connected to this sort of thing."

Dan nodded. "I see what you mean."

"I'm not sure you do."

Dan's eyes narrowed as his face showed confusion.

Jack took a quick drink from his mug, and turned back to Dakota Dan. "You remember how Bill Hickock got gunned down?"

"Sure do. Back in '76, up in Deadwood. Some cross–

eyed drifter back-shot him. Guess he was lookin' for a reputation, but they hung him for it."

"You remember his name?"

Dan thought for a moment or two. "Yup. He went by the name of Sutherland, Bill Sutherland. I remember it because I ran into a fella who played cards with the no-account a few days before he shot Hickock."

"You're right, Sutherland was the name he was using at the time, but he went by several names." His eyes drifted away, then back to Dan. "The name on his tombstone is Jack McCall."

Dan shook his head. "Is that what's troublin' you? Heck, partner, we've both got common names. Why do you think I go by Dakota? You know how many Dan Smiths are out there?" He gave another shake of the head. "It's the same with you. You're known as Dia-mondback McCall! Everybody knows that. And they know what kind of man you are." He followed those words with one firm nod.

Jack put his right hand on Dan's shoulder. "Thanks Dakota." Then he gave a couple of shakes of the head, and his face seemed to grow tense. "But I passed through Deadwood some years back." His eyes drifted away again. "A man there had the brass to ask me if that back-shooter was kin to me."

"He couldn't be?"

"Of course not! But I made up my mind right then that, somehow, I'd set things right. And, somehow, I'd make up for the stain that no-good put on my name."

"That explains a lot, partner." Dan's eyes seemed to go distant, like he was recollecting all the times he had seen Jack stand up against long odds. The distant expression soon disappeared, and he looked back to his friend. "Well, at least now I know why you have to try and right every wrong you see."

"I guess you're right about that."

Dan nodded and gave a half smile. "All right, Jack, we'll head back to Nogales and clear your name, soon as we finish our business for the chief."

Dan saw the troubled expression fade from his partner's face, and soon their Mexican breakfast arrived. But as they began eating, both Jack and Dan noticed that one of the cowboys at the bar was staring in their direction. Dan spoke while chewing. "That looks like trouble brewing, partner."

"Guess this is the day for it," Jack returned, as the cowpoke left his white Stetson on the bar, and began making his way through the tables. He stopped two steps before them. Jack simply kept eating, giving him but the slightest glance. The cowboy was only medium height, but stocky. He was wide of chest and seemed to be expanding it. Jack was reminded of a rooster trying to impress a hen. The cowhand wore a red plaid shirt, denim pants, but no gun.

After a quick turn back to his friends at the bar, perhaps for moral support, he spoke. His voice was low. His words came slow and deliberate. "I heard your friend call you Diamondback McCall. Is that true?"

Jack gave a single nod.

"You don't look so tough to me!"

"Then maybe you ought to look again." Jack spoke between bites, half ignoring him.

"You don't scare me, McCall. I've never lost a fight!"

Jack laid down his fork, and pushed back his chair a little. He looked up toward the hostile cowboy with impatience. "If you're looking for a fight, don't you think you ought to carry a gun?"

"I know you're fast with those fancy Colts. But how good are you with your fists?" He had a crazy look in his eyes. Jack couldn't help but wonder if it was from alcohol.

Jack abruptly stood up and stepped right up to the cowpoke. He had five inches and ten pounds on the ranchhand. The cowpuncher looked up at Jack's face and saw anger growing in his eyes. Momentarily, he glanced back at his fellow cowboys at the bar.

Jack also looked their way. "Your amigos?"

He nodded.

"Good. They'll be able to tell you all about this later, 'cause I don't think you're gonna remember much about it." Jack gave a half smile. "They can carry you out of here too."

Jack knew men who lose their tempers are easier foes. Their faces often give away their intentions. It wasn't that he couldn't hold his own in a slugfest—he had very fast hands and a punch like the kick of a mule—he was just smart enough to give himself a little edge.

The anger was quickly displayed in the cowboy's expression. A second later, he threw a wild right-hand punch. He swung his fist so hard and wide, that Jack had little problem deflecting it. Jack used his left forearm to block the blow and then added his own. He sunk a devastating right to the cowpoke's belly. That one blow caused him to double over, and then drop to his knees. Then, with his hands on the floor and his head hanging low, he coughed and gasped for air. Jack could see that he was the very picture of pain.

It was plain that he had had enough. Jack bent down, clasped the cowboy's upper right arm with both hands, and pulled him to his feet. He then had to nearly drag him across the floor to the bar. When he reached the other three cowpokes, he just pushed him toward them. As they grabbed their friend, Jack added, "Get him out of here. He's starting to get me riled." He turned away before any of them spoke.

On the way back to his table, Jack noted the other men at the nearby tables. The three men at the corner table were all smiling. They apparently enjoyed the entertainment. However, the man that sat alone between them and Dan had a different expression. He had a dead serious look and seemed to be studying him. When Jack reached Dan, the man quickly stood up and left.

Jack sat beside Dan and watched the exit of the

cowboys and the other man. He would remember him. Small and thin, with a bowler hat covering most of his sandy hair. There was something about his face that bothered him. Hard, cruel eyes, with a mouth to match. He wore a gray business suit but no holster. However, Jack detected a bulge beneath his jacket that was obviously a small-caliber pistol.

Dan had a bit of a grin. He managed to lose some of it before stating, "That feller wasn't any too friendly, either."

"This whole town seems a mite unfriendly to me, Dakota. Maybe we ought to be on our way."

Dan nodded, and they quickly finished breakfast. Between the suspicious man in the bowler and the bounty on his head, Jack thought it best to leave by the back door. Soon they made their way to the assay office and then across the street to the bank. Upon leaving the bank, Jack noted that the town had gotten busy. Both men wasted little time reaching their waiting mounts. They quickly untied the reins, and Jack dropped the bank book and that young gunslinger's pistol in his left saddlebag. Then they swung up into their saddles and spurred the horses to a trot.

This was the second time that Chief Tecanay had asked Jack to take a small amount of gold into town and make a deposit for the tribe at the bank. Jack would do just about anything for the chief and the Anasazi people. But both times he'd run into trouble. At least

Robert Middleton

this time they concluded business without Dan taking a bullet in the leg.

Before long they were out in the desert, leaving un-friendly Tucson behind.

Chapter Two

Conquistador

As the two men traveled their southerly route, Jack noted the sun had risen over his left shoulder and into the cloudless sky. The air, however, remained brisk. Dan, riding quietly to his right, had been content to hold the collar of his coat snug against his neck with his left hand, in an effort to fend off the cold. There was a stillness across the desert. No movement of wildlife or trace of wind. Just a stark scene of sand, brush, cactus, and the mountains looming in the distance.

During the couple of hours it took to reach the Papago village at Mission San Xavier, Jack had, on occasion, caught just a faint glimpse of a rider several miles ahead. It wouldn't ordinarily have bothered him, but the trouble he just had in town made him a little wary. He knew that most riders traveling south would be passing through the

Papago reservation. Still, he found himself feeling tense, his senses alerted.

When they rode into the village they saw the usual activity of everyday life and commerce. The vendors near the mission itself had their wares on display, and smoke rose from a couple of cooking fires, with the accompanying scent of burning mesquite. People of all ages moved about the scattered huts beyond the area of business.

Jack and Dan stopped their horses between the vendors and the mission entrance. At first, it all seemed routine. But then Jack saw a rider. Beyond the huts and down past the river, he could just make him out. As the rider passed through a gap between the trees that lined the Santa Cruz River he saw him clear enough. He also knew it had to be the same rider they had been following, for it was the man he'd seen just that morning. The man wearing the bowler.

Jack watched until there was no more sign of him. He was heading south. That made sense, but Jack didn't like coincidence. He gave another scan in that direction.

Dan noticed his partner's attention drawn to the rider. "You know that feller, Jack?"

"He was at the eatery."

"Some reason you're concerned with him? I mean, he can't be following us. He got here first."

"Maybe you're right, Dakota. I guess I'm just suspicious." What Dan said seemed obvious. Still, Jack found himself once again looking in that rider's direction.

With still no sign of him, he relaxed a little, and stepped down from his mount, as did Dan. They led their ponies to a rugged post by the mission's entrance. Dan then motioned toward the area of business with a tilt of the head. "I'm gonna find somebody to feed and water our ponies, Jack. I'll meet you inside, after."

Jack gave a single nod, and turned for the mission.

No matter how many times he visited the mission, Jack was always struck by its beauty. Classic Spanish architecture, with two great towers flanking the ornate facade. Still, to Jack's eyes, the true beauty was within the walls, and it had nothing to do with architecture. In one of the smaller rooms adjacent to the courtyard was the most beautiful girl he'd ever known. She taught school there, at least when the children could be spared from helping their families eke out an existence from the harsh land.

Jack quickly made his way through the large entryway and three adjoining rooms. Finding the door to the classroom ajar, he briefly stood in the doorway and simply watched her for a few moments. Fawn sat at her desk looking down at a tattered old book, alone in the empty classroom. Within seconds, sensing his presence, she raised her head, and their eyes met. Without speaking, they rushed toward each other, meeting midway alongside the students' tables and chairs. Jack smiled down at her and then lifted her by the waist, holding her before him. Her lovely face and gleaming dark eyes captivated him. He slowly pulled her close and kissed her.

After the long embrace, he set her down easy and watched her expression change. "I thought you were going to stay at the village for a while?" The corners of her mouth dipped, but the displeasure didn't seem entirely genuine.

He shrugged. "The chief asked me to do some business for him in town. You know I like to help out the tribe when I can."

She nodded, as her eyes betrayed the effort to look angry. "Well, be careful. That 'Wanted' poster has gotten around." Her face then showed only concern. "When are you going?"

He gave a slightly twisted smile. "Already been there. We're heading back to the village tonight."

She wore a look of shock and relief all at once. "And you didn't have any trouble?" Her voice had a clear ring of surprise. "Everyone's been saying how bountyhunters are on the prowl all over the territory these days, and a common sight in Tucson."

"Well, I'm afraid you're right about the bounty-hunters."

Her eyes narrowed and her hands moved to her hips. "What happened?"

"Let's just say it's time to get that price off my head."

At that moment Dan strolled into the classroom. Hearing those last few words, he approached them and added, "Yep, we're headin' down to Nogales to square Jack with the Federales."

"Then, I'm going with you." She said it in a way that left little question of her being serious.

"That might be dangerous, sweetheart. Besides, what about your class?"

She smiled and made a broad gesture toward the empty room. "I haven't had a pupil in almost a week. They're needed in the fields." She gave one very firm nod. "I'm going!"

Jack loved everything about Fawn, even her independence. He knew there was little point in trying to dissuade her once her mind was made up. Still, he didn't like putting her at risk. He looked briefly into her lovely eyes and gave a reluctant nod.

They spent the remainder of the day around the mission and managed a siesta in preparation for the coming trek. With the setting sun, they saddled up and headed southeast. It took most of the night to reach the Anasazi village—a secret, subterranean city, unknown to the world above. It was a long, cold ride under bright stars and no moon. As unpleasant as it was, the trio didn't complain. They knew it was simply necessary to make the trip by night. No one could possibly follow them in the darkness.

With less than an hour before first light glowed to the east, they finally made their way into the narrow boxed canyon that led to the cavern's stone entrance door. Once inside, they first stopped at the stable and tended to the horses. After passing through the second stone door, they began descending the two long ladders.

The city was at the end of its day. Darkness gave a murky view of the huge cavern. Less than a dozen people remained in the courtyard. They too, would soon be retiring to their dwellings built one upon another. Few of the stone and masonry structures that lined the cavern walls still had light glowing from their single windows. Before long, only tiny streams of sunlight would prevent total darkness. Shafts of light manage to find their way through the many cracks in the cavern roof. These cracks, of course, also allow the smoke to escape. That smoke could be seen during the day. So, the city lives by night.

The fact that Jack and company had just traveled all night helped the adjustment to the upside-down time of the world below. Tired, they would have little trouble sleeping the first of the Anasazi nights. Jack had found that it took a while for the body to get used to the backward routine, but this time they wouldn't be staying long enough for that.

Chota, as well as several in the village, saw them stepping off the last ladder as they reached the courtyard. He hurried over to them, a smile across his face as he fondly nodded at his friends.

Chota was a slightly built man. Like most in the village, he wore alabaster-colored clothes that were a bit on the short side. But the single hawk's feather atop his long hair indicated he was an emissary for the chief and at that moment he spoke for Chief Tecanay. "Chief wants to see you. All of you."

They all smiled and returned the nod. Chota then turned to lead the way. As the three followed, it was evident that the tribe thought of them as nearly one of them. There were people by the fountain and the ceremonial Kiva. They greeted them with smiles and a sense of welcome. Of course all three had come to feel the same way about the village. Chota continued to walk toward the dark side of the huge cavern, and the Chief's dwelling.

Within the large, bottom-level structure, a small fire still flickered in a round hearth against the far wall. The last smoldering embers of the day. Chief Tecanay sat beside the dwindling fire on a thick mat and looked up as his visitors arrived. He motioned them in and then pointed toward the four mats in front of him.

Chota was to Tecanay's far right. Fawn, Jack, and Dan sat to Chota's right, and he turned their way to translate for the chief. "It is good to have you all back with us." He then looked straight at Jack and Fawn. "It is always good to see you together. You belong together and you belong here."

Jack and Fawn exchanged slightly embarrassed smiles and the chief continued.

"I hope that one day you will find that all you need is here with us." He glanced Dan's way to assure him that his words were meant for him, as well. He then turned and reached for a long dull object laying on the stone floor. When he brought it around and held it up before him, his three guests leaned forward to get a better look. It was a sword with an ornate silver and ivory handle. The blade was concealed within a dark leather scabbard, trimmed with more silver. A Spanish sword of the Cortez era. In fact, Jack recognized it as a Toledo Sword, prized for the quality of its steel. "This belonged to an outsider who became one of us. He was my great, great grandfather."

Fawn was doing her best to study the ancient weapon in the dim light. She looked up at the chief. "How did he come to you?"

Chota translated the question, but Chief Tecanay seemed to already sense what her curiosity compelled her to ask. "Generations ago, three of our hunters found a soldier dying in the desert. He was lying in his own blood and had an Apache arrow in his back. They carried him back here. Then one of our young women tended to the wound and nursed him to health." The chief briefly smiled at Jack and Fawn, and then went on. "They fell in love and married. He was then one of us. They were happy together and had two sons. She was my great, great grandmother."

Somehow, Jack had assumed that the three of them were the first outsiders to ever come to the hidden city. He considered why the chief chose to tell the story and thought about that conquistador, so long ago. With the Apache after him above and the Anasazi unwilling to let him leave, he had no choice in the matter. He had to stay. Still, Jack knew the true meaning of the chief's story. The world above is fraught with danger, hardship, and uncertainty. And life within the secret village could only be described as harmonious. It was the chief's wisdom and kindness that prompted him to share it. The message wasn't lost on Jack, but it went against his thirst for adventure, and the freedom he felt on the trail.

While Jack pondered the small piece of history he'd just heard, Fawn was more interested in the actual relic. She approached the chief without speaking and tried to examine the sword more closely. Tecanay smiled, passed it to her, and she returned the smile.

Jack and Dan soon found themselves watching Fawn as she pored over every inch of the heavy weapon. Dan then turned to his partner. "You two gonna settle down here one day?"

Jack's expression did little to disguise the doubt. "Do you think I could stay down here for good?"

"Nope. Not now. But I've known a few men with reputations. It comes with a mighty high price. You kill them, or they kill you. And it never stops, partner."

Jack lowered his head a little, then slowly turned to watch Fawn. She was staring at the back side of the leather sheath. After a moment he gave a nod. "I know."

The light grew ever dimmer, and soon the chief's guests left to get some sleep. Chota bid them good night midway across the courtyard, and within minutes Jack and company were stretched out on their soft woven mats within their own quarters.

On the far right side of the room, Dan was soon asleep, accompanied by his usual grunting and whizzing sounds. On the opposite side, Jack and Fawn simply lay silently side by side, only a few feet apart, with their eyes wide open. It was the chief's story, and perhaps even more what Dan had said that weighed on Jack's mind. Killing was indeed a high price for freedom. Even killing in self-defense can haunt a man of conscience. Jack had always managed to be on the right side of a fight. And he knew the men he had killed were killers themselves. Still, he knew that when he left the Anasazi village, sooner or later, he'd have to kill again.

He was glad when Fawn rolled toward him and interrupted his troubling thoughts. "You ever heard of Canon De Oro Del Diablo?"

"The Canyon of the Devil's Gold?" He shook his head. "I don't think so. Why?"

"It's one of those ancient legends of gold and treasure that the conquistadors tried to find."

"Like El Dorado?"

She nodded.

"So, what about it?"

"That soldier"—she moved closer and spoke softer—"he found it."

Chapter Three

Nogales

As the fire lights brought morning to the village, darkness descended on the world above. Not long after breakfast, Jack, Dan, and Fawn bid their Anasazi friends good-bye. It was a long ride to Nogales and Jack wanted to get on with it.

Another cold night greeted the threesome when they left the hidden city behind. Chota and Chief Tecanay had accepted their short visit cordially enough, even though they couldn't really understand the lure of the outside world. Of course it was simply freedom. And that's what Jack felt as he once again headed for the trail. It caused him to doubt if he could ever be content to live out his days in the cavern city.

While leading their horses out of the boxed canyon, Jack looked up and marveled at the bright stars. It was another moonless night. Even as their eyes adjusted to the night, they could see only a few feet into the murky darkness. There was no wind, but there was a brisk chill to the air. At the end of the canyon, they coaxed their ponies down into the rocky gully, and turned south. Soon they were out on the desert plain, riding side by side, and negotiating the terrain as best they could with minimal light.

Fawn was riding between the two men; Jack was to her right. He turned her way. "Did you tell Dan what you found on that scabbard?"

Dan had been hunched over a little, bracing against the chill air. He sat up straight with curiosity. "What about that scabbard?"

"Well, that conquistador scratched out an account of his expedition to find gold in a secret canyon on the back of that leather sheath."

"Oh, I think I've heard of that one. The Devil's gold, right?" He seemed to dismiss it as nonsense.

"That's right."

"And it's supposed to be some sacred Apache canyon and of course, no one's ever come out alive."

"Well, at least one did, Dan," Fawn stated matter-of-factly.

"You mean he really found it?"

"That's what it said. There's even a map."

Dan's voice suddenly sounded excited. "We goin' after it, partner?"

Jack didn't seem to share Dan's excitement. "No. I don't think so."

Fawn turned to Jack. "Why not? We went all the way to Vera Cruz after gold and this canyon's not that far from here." There was disappointment in the tone.

"That was different."

"How?"

"That Aztec gold was lost and the Aztecs who owned it are long gone. This is Apache gold. I won't steal from anyone."

There was no answer from Fawn or Dan right away, then Fawn replied, "It wasn't so much the gold that intrigued me. It was trying to find it."

"I understand, but try explaining that to the Apache, if we got that close."

"I guess you're right, but remember how exciting it was hunting for treasure in Vera Cruz."

"Exciting? We barely lived through it. Didn't even come away with the gold." Jack loved her spirit, however that venture to Vera Cruz was one close call after another.

"But we found it." She was justly proud of that fact.

There was a tinge of pride in Dan's voice too. "We also saw to it those dirty, gun-runnin' pirates ended up in a Mexican jail."

"Well, that's the best part of it. Knowing the Federales sent Captain LeBoux and his cutthroats to a Mexican prison."

After a moment or two, Fawn looked to Dan. You could hear a hint of worry as she spoke. "What about the Federales in Nogales? You think you'll have any trouble straightening out this bounty business?"

"Nope. I just need to find my old amigo Sargento Ramirez. He lives a few miles south of town. He headed up the local Federales, back when I was a deputy, and I helped him out a few times. He's a good friend and owes me a favor."

With that answer she seemed content. They rode on through the still darkness, with the temperature growing even colder than the previous night. They finally entered Nogales a couple of hours before sunup.

Darkness was nearly total in the sleeping border town. The only light that could be seen was from a window of the tiny Hotel Nogales.

All three were cold, and Fawn had by that point been reduced to shivers. It was quickly decided to roust the hotel owner and see about getting her under some blankets. Dan pressed on, wanting to reach Senor Ramirez early, before he left his home.

Jack and Fawn tied off their mounts in front of the adobe and brick hotel and went to the arched, wooden door. It took some repeated knocking and pounding to make the owner answer the door. All was concluded pleasantly, however, once Jack offered to pay enough extra pesos.

After signing the register, he wasted little time in putting Fawn to bed, and added all the blankets from the second bed. He then stretched out on that other bed and watched her in the dimness. The shivers soon ended and she drifted off to sleep. Jack knew there would be little time for sleep. Dan would most likely be back in a couple of hours. So, he didn't even bother to remove his boots, but just set his hat beside him on the bed and closed his eyes.

Jack's brief slumber ended abruptly. With the arrival of first light, there was a sudden clamor of voices and footsteps just outside their door. The sounds of many men and the clicking of rifles being cocked could also be heard encircling the little hotel. Jack was on his feet in a second. He went to the one tiny window facing rearward, for a quick look.

It was the Mexican Army.

Then, from the other side of the door came a strong and agitated voice. "You are surrounded, *señor*! Come out unarmed! Come out now!"

Even if Fawn wasn't there, he would have to comply. He was hopelessly outgunned. With her looking to him with terrified eyes, he removed his holster without hesitation. Jack motioned for her to stay put on the bed, as he went for the door. "I'm coming out, unarmed." He slowly opened the door and raised his hands. In the narrow hallway, three soldiers greeted him by raising their rifles at his head. There were more troops in the small lobby, accompanied by a stout and stern-looking corporal.

As Jack was escorted to the jail, all of the Federales who had surrounded the hotel joined in the procession. Jack was slightly amused to have twenty-odd men aiming their weapons at an unarmed man. Evidently, his reputation didn't stop at the border.

The old jailhouse was less than two blocks away. It was behind the courtyard of the town's administering offices. A simple square structure made of brick and adobe with three-foot-thick walls. Iron bars faced the courtyard. Within the cell was a ten-foot-square space containing one occupant. He was old, bearded, and dirty. His clothes were nearly rags and he shivered uncontrollably, huddled in the far left corner.

The corporal led the way to the austere jail cell. He unlocked the iron door, stood aside, and let his troops nudge Jack inside with their rifles. The iron door slammed shut and the corporal secured the lock.

It had all been very businesslike, without a word being spoken. Perhaps the Federales thought that Jack didn't understand Spanish. Perhaps they didn't care. Mexican authorities were known to deal out fast and harsh punishment and they didn't always bother with formalities, such as a judge, a jury, or even charging a prisoner with a crime.

It wasn't hard to figure how they knew he was there. It was the hotel register. Jack did think it odd that it happened so fast. He wondered how the local police had checked the hotel records, rounded up the Federales, and had them surround the hotel, all by sunup. Bad luck, he finally concluded. He had planned on turning himself in and then letting Dan and his amigo straighten out the matter. Being brought to jail at gunpoint would only make him look more guilty.

With the withdrawal of the troops, Fawn came running across the courtyard. They met at the cell door. There were tears flowing from her pretty eyes. She clasped the bars, he put his hands over hers, and they kissed between the bars. Jack wiped the tears from her cheek and managed a smile. "Don't worry about this. Dan will be along soon to get me out."

"You really think so?"

"Sure." He wasn't actually as confident as he let on. "You better go on back to the hotel and wait for Dan. I'll be fine."

His reassurance quelled her tears. She nodded and headed back to await Dan's return.

As Jack watched her leaving the courtyard, the old man at the back of the cell spoke very softly. His teeth chattered a little from the cold and he had a slight Spanish accent. "You really think you're getting out of here, *señor*?"

Jack turned to face the frail old hombre sitting in the corner on a small blanket, with another one draped over his shoulders.

"I've got a friend. He has an amigo in the Federales."

"That is good, *señor*. Why did they arrest you?"

"They say I gunned down two unarmed men, here in Nogales."

"*Si*, I heard about that." He studied Jack more closely. "You are the one they call Diamondback."

Jack nodded. "McCall."

"I know about you. People talk. I don't think you would have to do such a thing? They say you are *muy rapido*! They also say you have honor."

Jack returned a nod in appreciation. "So, what are you in for?"

"For stealing a horse."

Jack merely gave him a stare and turned away. Horse thieves were looked on with contempt by most men. Jack was no exception.

The old man spoke to Jack's back. "Señor McCall, I will die in this place. I cannot survive in the cold. I'm not a well man."

Jack looked back at the frail old man shivering in the corner. He did, indeed, look to be sickly. He wondered how long the old-timer would last in such conditions. "When I get out, I'll talk to the authorities. Maybe they'll let you have more blankets."

"You can buy my release for one thousand pesos, Señor McCall."

Jack returned a puzzled look. "Why would I do that?"

"Because if you do, I'll tell you where we hid the strongbox."

"What strongbox?"

"The one we stole from the Federales."

"You're not making much sense."

The old man gave a couple of nods. "There were three of us and we took it from the officers' quarters when the troops were on patrol. It was easy, only one guard and he was drunk. That was nine years ago. We hid the strongbox about an hour's ride from here and then crossed the border. We planned to come back a few months later, after they stopped looking for us. But a U.S. posse caught up with us first. We were also wanted for rustling cattle in Arizona. They gave us ten years at Yuma, but they let me out early for good behavior and they figured I was about to die anyway."

"So, you came back to get the loot and stole a horse along the way." Jack shook his head. "Doesn't sound like you learned much."

"I know what you think of me, but you can have the money. I'll tell you where it is if you just get me out of here." The old man was pleading. "I'll tell you, Mr. Mc-Call, because you're a man of honor."

"I'm a man of my word, but I haven't given it to you."

"Get me out and the money is yours."

Jack had no interest in anything stolen. Still, he considered the merits of the old bandit's offer. He liked the idea of returning the chest to its rightful owners. And a little treasure hunt might just make up for Fawn's disappointment in not seeking the Apache gold. There was also the matter of the old prisoner. Despite being nothing but a common thief, Jack couldn't just let him die. He gave the frail hombre a nod. "All right. You tell me where it is. If you're telling me the truth, I'll come back and buy your release."

A smile spread across the old-timer's face. He motioned Jack closer and softly told him where to find the buried strongbox.

Chapter Four

Self-Defense

It had taken only minutes for the old man to pass along directions to the buried payroll. They sealed their agreement by simply shaking hands. Two hours later Dan arrived with Fawn.

Jack could tell by their expressions that it had gone well. He greeted his partner with an outstreched arm through the bars. "So, I take it you found Sargento Ramirez?"

"Yup. He's talking to his corporal right now."

"You have any trouble convincing him it was a fair fight?"

"Nope. He never understood why a man with your reputation would have to shoot unarmed men. But since Foley was a witness, and we lit out, it made things look bad. So, I told him why you had to leave so fast, that you went to rescue two young boys."

"And that's all it took?"

"Well, I also reminded him of when I saved his life."

Up to that point, Fawn had been content to just listen. "You really saved his life?"

Dakota pointed to his left shoulder. "I got between Ramirez and a bullet heading his way. I think that made us friends."

Jack smiled and gave a shake of the head. "You've got a mighty convincing way of making friends. It wasn't that long ago that you took a slug intended for me."

"Yeah." The corners of Dan's mouth curled up. "There's gotta be an easier way to make friends."

"Next time, why don't you try buying somebody a beer?"

Dan answered with a couple of nods and a little grin.

About ten minutes later three Federales entered the courtyard and headed for the tiny jail cell. The sergeant, carrying Jack's guns and holster, led the way. Close behind was the corporal, along with a private, who was carrying a rifle on his right shoulder. Dan and Fawn stepped aside while the corporal brushed by his sergeant to unlock the cell door and pull it open. He said nothing, but simply turned away and left with the private in tow. Jack stepped through the doorway and offered a hand to Sargento Ramirez, a middle-aged gent with a handsome face behind a wide black mustache.

After handing over Jack's weapons he gave a firm hand-shake and added, "You are free to go, *señor*. My amigo, Dan, has given his word that it was self-defense." He gave a nod in Dakota's direction. "That is good enough for me."

"*Gracias*, Sargento. I'm in your debt."

"*De nada*. But watch your back, Señor McCall. It will take some time to recall those Wanted posters."

Jack nodded and added, "*Hasta luego!*"

The sergeant bid *adios* to the three and they made their way back to their horses. As they swung up into the saddles, Dan looked up and down the street. Businesses were opening and people were freely moving about. One well-armed gringo was just a few storefronts behind them and he seemed to be watching them. Dan shook his head. "Partner. I think my Federale friend is right. You ought to lay low for a while."

"Maybe so, but not quite yet." Jack turned his horse and nudged him ahead. They both sided him as he headed up the street. "I kinda remember a cafe by a hardware store toward the end of this street."

Dan looked Jack's way. "We gonna stop for vittles?" It was obvious from his expression that he was hungry.

Jack smiled. "Okay, but I need to pick up something in that hardware store."

Fawn wondered what he needed from a hardware store, but was more concerned with getting him out of town quickly. "Maybe Dan and I should head for that cafe while you're doing that. That will save a little time."

That seemed reasonable to Jack. He gave a nod and they rode on. Within minutes they were approaching the two businesses and Jack looked along the storefronts on both sides of the street. It was fairly quiet but there were three horses with saddles from across the border tied off in front of a cantina, just past the cafe.

They pulled their horses to a halt and stepped down onto the dusty street. As Jack led his mount to the hitching rail and Fawn and Dan did the same, he turned to them. "I'll meet you inside in a few minutes." Then he looked at Fawn and smiled fondly. "Now, don't talk to any strangers."

She simply returned the smile and headed for the cafe with Dan on her heels.

Jack watched them until they disappeared within the eatery, then turned for the hardware store. The name FERRETERIA NOGALES stood just above the open door. He walked in and perused the fair-sized store. It was well stocked with everything you'd find in a store in Tucson. What he was looking for was a basic tool. They would need a shovel to dig up that strongbox, and he spotted a short-handled spade in the far corner. It took but minutes to deal with the cashier, return to his horse, and then tie the three-foot long shovel behind his saddle.

As Jack started the dozen or so steps to the cafe named Rosita's he became alert. It was a well-worn adobe structure with peeling white paint and one tiny window on each side of the open door. But that was unnoticed by him. He could hear three men inside and their voices clearly rang of trouble. It wasn't the first time that Fawn's striking beauty had attracted the worst sort of men's interest. The result, however, was the same. It wasn't something Jack took kindly to and he was the wrong man to anger.

By the time he reached the entrance his expression had turned to stone, with his eyes narrow and cold. He paused briefly in the doorway. On the left was the kitchen, with a very nervous cook and waiter peering carefully over a masonry counter. Tables with their accompanying chairs lined the other three walls, with a small open space in the middle. Fawn and Dan had chosen the table in the far right corner. They were seated behind their table and facing the entrance. The three men that were facing them were leaning over the table, taunting Fawn, and ignoring Dan. They had their backs to the entrance and Jack. They were also well armed with the holsters of professional gunmen.

Jack was always under control, even though these three gunmen were spewing slurs and suggestive language toward the woman he loved. Despite his growing anger he let things play out a little.

When the three men seemed to be at the point where they were going from mere words to actually putting their hands on her, Dan suddenly stood up. "This is as far as it goes! You boys ought to know you're about to go up against somebody way faster than the three of you!"

The threesome glared at Dakota for a moment and started to laugh. As the laughter petered out, the man in the center gave Dan another look. The man was about thirty, average height and he wore a black Stetson tilted forward on his thin unshaven face. He wore his gun low and his voice was equally low. "You, Pops?" He managed a crooked smile.

Dan shook his head and pointed toward the doorway. "No. Him!"

As the three gunhands turned around, Jack walked straight for them. With three steps between them, he stopped. For a moment there was the usual sizing up on each side. Jack noted the man in the center was a bit older than his amigos. They all had the hard, steady eye of the gunslinger. The one to Jack's right was staring down at his Colts. He then gave a quick glance to his friends. "Diamondback McCall." There was no alarm in the tone; he simply acknowleged it.

Many times in the past, men would gladly back down when they knew whom they were up against. Even professionals like these hombres. But those Wanted posters seemed to have changed all that. With a tarnished reputation, Jack would likely have to fight.

The other two gunmen were also unimpressed by their opponent. The center man did the talking. "That true, mister?"

Jack returned a single nod.

"Well, there's Wanted posters for you plastered all over this town."

Jack gave another nod. "But those posters were a mistake. The Mexican authorities are recalling them."

All three wore a look of pure skepticism, but again the center hombre spoke. "So, it's just a big mistake!" All three saw humor in it.

"Well, it's not as big as the one you're making."

The humor disappeared from his face. "Why don't you just drop that gunbelt, McCall?"

"Why don't I just drop the three of you instead?"

With a startled expression he fired back, "You ain't got a chance against us. And we're collecting that reward, one way or another."

"If you boys really want a fight, you're gonna get your just reward, but it won't be coming in pesos." There was the ring of finality in the tone.

"I guess you don't know who we are."

Jack didn't care. He was tired of the tough talk, and it showed.

"Ned Flynn's the name!" He said that with a good deal of pride, then glanced to his right. "This is Tom Searles!" He then looked the other way. "And John T. Sloan!" He expected their names to impress.

Of course Jack had heard of them. They were well-known gunslingers. Fast, but not that fast. He simply gave a couple of nods and added, "I'll pass that information on to the cemetery."

The time for banter seemed to be over. Jack motioned for Dan and Fawn to move out of the line of fire. They scrambled out from behind the table and dashed into the corner to their left.

Jack knew these men were close to slapping iron. It

wasn't just because they thought there was reward money. It was more simple than that. These were gunmen that liked what they did. They liked to kill, and were proud of it. And killing a man like Diamondback McCall would enhance their reputation.

Jack got no pleasure from killing. Even men like these three. But he was resigned to the fact that if they wanted a fight, that's just what they'd get. "All right boys. It's up to you." Jack flicked his eyes toward the doorway. "Walk out of here nice and easy, or grab those shooters and end up leaving feet first!"

Jack had no sooner said those words than they went for their guns. They were professionals and had practiced at drawing on cue. A slight gesture on the part of the center man caused all three to spring to action. They moved in perfect sync, drawing at the exact same time. Three shots blasted out in rapid succession, and the three gunmen dropped to the floor, also at the exact same time. Jack had put one bullet apiece between the eyes of each man. They hadn't even cleared leather before he ended their killing, greed, and wasted lives.

The sound of three shots fired nearly simultaneously bounced about the tiny cafe. While the smoke lingered in the air, Jack stood motionless for several moments. A grisly sight, even for a man who'd seen it all before. After a shake of the head, he spun his Colts back into their holsters and turned to Fawn. She seemed in shock, the color drained from her pretty face, tears welling up.

Dan had witnessed enough killing in his life to know

that it was sometimes necessary. And he knew it probably wasn't over. Even though these three killers gave his partner no choice in the matter, there would likely be others to try to avenge their deaths. Then there was the grim reminder of all this. The faces of three more dead men that his friend would carry with him for the rest of his life.

Jack went to Fawn and held her. She trembled in his arms. If there were appropriate words, they failed him.

Chapter Five

Persona Non Grata

It took less than five minutes for the Federales to arrive. They then quickly formed into a single line of infantry with all rifles trained on Cafe Rosita's front door. Jack didn't wait to be called out. He handed Dan his holster, raised his hands, and slowly walked out to be taken away. Once again, all twenty-odd men kept their rifles pointed his way as they escorted him back to jail.

It was done with the same silent efficiency as before. But as they crossed the courtyard and the small jail cell came into view, something was different. The old man was gone. All that remained were his blankets heaped in the corner.

Once Jack was ushered inside, the corporal secured the lock and he and the troops withdrew. Jack was then left to wonder about that old-timer and his own fate. An hour passed, then another.

Finally, Sargento Ramirez, along with Dan and Fawn entered the courtyard. Dan still held Jack's holster, but all three wore solemn expressions. Jack waited with his hands clasping the bars and received a cold look with the arrival of the sergeant.

It should have been a simple matter to resolve. There were four witnesses, including the two locals that watched from within the kitchen. However, it was evident that Señor Ramirez was quite angry. For a moment or two he stood there stiffly, with brooding eyes and a clenched jaw. He then, with some reluctance, produced the key from his pocket and unlocked the metal door. He opened it only partially, and stood in the opening. "This is not Tombstone, Señor McCall! We don't allow shooting and killing in our pueblos. This is where we live and now our women are afraid to leave their homes."

Jack dropped his head some.

"I warned you not to stay in Nogales." He glanced back at Dakota. "Señor Dan is my amigo, but the people here are angry and you are no longer welcome." Ramirez stepped aside and allowed Jack to exit the cell. He then gave a terse motion with his head to move along toward the street.

As they walked across the courtyard, Jack considered recent events. He knew the sergeant was right. He had lingered in town too long and had the bad luck to run into the wrong men. In fact, luck had not been on his side lately. It was starting to bother him. Two men wanted to fight in Tucson. Then the Federales found him at the hotel. And the gunplay that morning at the cafe. Along with that, he thought of the suspicious man in the bowler and now the old man was gone from the jail cell.

Jack wanted to ask about the missing prisoner, but his attention was suddenly diverted. Once they reached the street they were met with mounted Federales, nearly thirty of them, led by that stern-faced corporal. He also held the reins of the three gringos' horses. Somehow the disappearance of the old man seemed less important. They were being escorted out of town, by force if necessary, and were simply expected to comply. Without a single word from anyone, Jack and company took the waiting reins, swung into their saddles and headed out of town. They were, of course, closely followed by the entire complement of troops.

Once they were beyond the town streets they headed north. Not because that was where Jack wanted to go, but rather because that's where they were expected to go. When they crossed the railroad tracks that ran just north of the border, their escorts stopped. They stayed and watched the trio until they were a couple of miles within Arizona, then turned back to Nogales.

Jack noted the soldiers heading south and turned to Fawn. She was riding between the two men with her head tilted downward and tears in the corners of her pretty eyes. It was obvious that she was having a tough time dealing with what she had seen that morning. "Unfortunate business, those three men at the cafe. I'm sorry you were so close to it."

She looked over to him, trying not to show just how troubled she actually was. "I've seen you handle men before, but you've never had to kill them."

"You think I handled it poorly?"

"No, it's not that. There was no talking them out of it. They would have killed you, if they could have. Of course you had to defend yourself. But . . ."

"But death is grim enough without being so unnecessary."

"And without seeing it personally."

He nodded.

Dan had seen enough hired guns to recognize a simple fact. The death of those three killers would doubtless save innocent people's lives. And the even simpler fact that they had it coming. That was the harsh truth of the matter and he wouldn't brood over it. He looked across to his partner, wanting to change the subject. "I'm afraid this trip only half worked, partner. We might have got that reward off your head, but we didn't make any friends south of the border. Don't think we better head back this way anytime soon."

"They made that point plenty clear. Think they call it, persona non grata." He managed a little smile. "Can't remember being run out of a town by the Army before."

Dan just returned a shake of the head.

Jack glanced Fawn's way, noting her same look of dismay. "It's too bad, actually. I got wind of a buried strongbox about an hour's ride into Mexico."

Both Fawn and Dan were giving Jack hard stares, with questioning eyes.

"It's true. That old man who shared the cell with me told me about it and where it was.

"Why would he do that?" Some of the pain disappeared from Fawn's face, replaced with doubt.

"I promised to buy his way out of jail, if it was really there. You see, it was payroll money. He and two other hombres stole it from the Federales nine years ago."

After exchanging nods with Dan, she turned to Jack. "Well, I think we should do it."

"Go after the treasure?"

She nodded.

"What about the Federales?"

"Don't you see? If we return that money, it fixes everything."

"What if the Army finds us first?"

"They won't. We'll stay far from town, until we bring in the strongbox. Then we'll be heroes."

Jack didn't share her optimism. It seemed risky and he was in the middle of a run of bad luck. But there was now something of a glow in her eyes, where sadness had been moments earlier. That was worth the risk to him. And he wasn't about to disappoint her, after what she'd just been through. "You up for this crazy venture, Dakota?"

Jack watched Dan's eyes grow narrow and his mouth curl into a twisted frown as he mulled it over. Like his friend, Dan saw it as a high-risk scheme. He finally gave in to a single nod. "Well, partner, I said we'd come down here and clear your name. I can't think of another way of doin' it."

"Me either." Jack pulled his mount to a halt, and pointed southeast. "All right. Let's go find it."

Chapter Six

Treasure Hunt

It was another day that wouldn't quite warm up. No clouds appeared above, just the sun unable to overcome the chill of a stiff breeze out of the east, and they were riding right into it. Ahead was Patagonia Mountain. The plan was to ride in the general direction of the mountain and then turn south. That would put some miles between them and Nogales and the Federales before crossing the border. About three hours would bring them far enough back into Mexico to pick up the trail described by the old prisoner.

Those miles passed uneventfully. They didn't catch sight of a single person. In fact, the only living creatures seen were an occasional high-flying bird and one distant coyote. That was of some relief to Jack because he still had an uneasy feeling caused from his steady run of bad

luck. He tried not to dwell on it. Instead, he made an effort to appreciate the rugged terrain. In the distance and
to their left was Patagonia Mountain. The course they
took kept them parallel to it. They rode on nearly due
south, traversing hills thick with sage brush and crossing several washes lined with sand and stones. It was a
tough route for their mounts, with little flat ground, and
the animals were tiring from the constant climbing and
descending. The trio continued on until Jack noted the
approaching trail described by the old-timer.

Before taking the trail's southeast turn, Jack pulled
Chilco to a halt, and the others followed suit. He looked
at Fawn and Dan to his right. "I recognize this from what
that old man told me." He pointed to his left, adding,
"We'll follow the trail around the left side of that big hill.
Then we should see a rocky pass that leads into a valley.
The strongbox is supposed to be buried about halfway
into that valley at the foot of a giant Saguaro."

"How far you figure that is, partner?"

"Less than an hour."

Dan stepped down from his pony. "Well, we ought to
let these horses rest a while before we go on." While
Jack and Fawn also dismounted, Dan went for his can-
teen, pulled off his hat, and poured a little water in it.
After giving his pony a drink, he tended to the other
two animals.

Jack and Fawn left Dan to his work and went to the
other side of one of the very large rocks nearby that
made up much of the area's landscape. With Dan just

out of sight, Jack took her hand and turned her so her back was touching the huge rock. He leaned against the rock, his hands flanking her shoulders, and slowly drew closer to her. Their lips met and she pulled him tight by the neck. Before Dan could interrupt the tender moment, Jack moved his head back a bit and gazed into her most-appealing eyes. "I love you," tumbled out before he knew he was going to say it.

"I love you too!" Her eyes seemed to sparkle; then she shivered a little from the chilly wind.

He wrapped her in his arms, holding her snugly only partly because of the cold. "Are you okay to go on?" His words were nearly whispered.

She pushed back some and looked firmly up at him. "Of course! I'm starting to get excited about this. Aren't you?"

He released the embrace while giving his shoulders a shrug. "I guess this treasure hunt has helped get your mind off of this morning, at least some. That's good. But I can't help wondering what happened to that old man in the cell. I made him a promise and now he's gone."

"You think something bad happened? You think he could have died?"

"That's possible, of course. He didn't look too good."

She shook her head. "I don't think so. They probably took him to see a doctor. Don't you think?" She smiled in her reassuring way. "Don't worry. I bet he's all right. You'll be able to keep your promise to him and return the stolen money to the Federales too."

She had a way of making things seem so simple. He found himself nodding. "Then I guess we'd better go get that treasure."

They saddled up and began following the trail. At least it was more level, making it far easier on the horses. The trail skirted that large hill and soon after veered toward a fairly narrow pass, punctuated with more huge gray rocks. Within minutes they were beginning to enter the pass. The great rocks caused the riders to negotiate around them because of their sheer number. Fawn was between the two men; Jack was on her right. At the same time, he and Dan turned to each other with similar looks of concern. "Heck of a place for an ambush, partner." Dan put his right hand on the handle of his Colt.

"If you were looking to bushwhack somebody, this would be the perfect place."

"Glad you approve, cowboy!" shouted a man from just behind the tall gray rock just ahead and to Jack's right. It was a familiar voice, the voice of Captain LeBoux.

At that very instant the horses stopped short and their ears darted forward from the sound of LeBoux and the other twelve men suddenly swinging their rifles at Jack and company from five different directions. Each man was using the rocks as cover, aiming the weapons at their prey without exposing much of themselves in the process. There was also one man atop a flat rock behind them who was pointing his Winchester squarely at Jack's back.

Jack knew from the sounds all around him that it was a hopeless situation. So did Dan. As he and his partner raised their hands, Jack heard the footsteps of one of the men from behind approaching on his right side. He stopped, looked up at Jack, and pointed the barrel of his rifle straight at his face. "I'd like to kill you right now, but there's no profit in it."

It was a serious situation, and Jack had little doubt that the man was deadly serious. A man capable of cruel deeds. That was how he impressed Jack. The same impression he had the first time he saw him in the cafe in Tucson. The man in the bowler. And it was just starting to make a little sense. It hadn't been a matter of bad luck. The events were beginning to add up.

It was apparent that LeBoux was at the heart of the conspiracy. And Jack also recognized a couple of the other men peering around their protecting rocks as members of his ship's crew, including his first mate. So, it wasn't a real surpise when another familar face appeared. As the captain walked out into the open between two rocks to Jack's right, the old man from the jail followed him. The rags had been replaced by gray Mexican riding clothes, but it was the same man. LeBoux had lost most of his nautical garb; he now wore a pale blue shirt over brown trousers and chaps. The big man still donned a full black beard, and atop his dark hair was his usual blue and white captain's cap.

The old-timer walked by the captain and up to Jack's left. "I'll take those *pistolas*, *señor*. *Muy despacio!* My amigo behind you can't miss at that distance." He held out his left hand.

Jack complied.

Once he tucked the two Colts behind his belt, the old-timer added, "The rifle too."

Again, Jack did as directed. Then the old man disarmed Dan in the same manner.

With Jack and Dan unarmed, the man in the bowler let the barrel of his rifle point downward, and stepped back some. At the same time the old man rejoined LeBoux. The rest of the men stayed at their positions, keeping the long guns aimed at Jack.

At that point LeBoux seemed relaxed, and walked closer to Jack. "This time I've got the drop on you, cowboy. Things have changed a little, wouldn't you say?"

"I don't know. Land or sea, you're still nothing but a pirate."

"Mighty tough talk for a man in your postion. I could kill you with the snap of my fingers. And after what you did to me in Vera Cruz, I think maybe I will."

Jack thought back to his run-in with LeBoux down in Mexico. The captain had learned of their map to a treasure beneath the waves and sailed after them to the site of the sunken island. Jack had dived down to find the lost Aztec pyramid, and while he secured a rope about the disk-shaped golden sun that rested atop the submerged temple, LeBoux and his pirates moved in. They ambushed the treasure seekers at sea, took the golden disk, and left them for dead, miles from shore. It took the clever mind of Fawn and Jack's ability to play out a bluff to later reverse the situation, but now it was, once again, LeBoux's game. "It's not revenge you want, or I'd already be dead."

"Don't be so sure, cowboy. I've got plenty of reason to want you dead." Anger flushed his face as he took a step closer and gave Jack an irritated stare. "You took everything I had and left me and my first mate treading water in Vera Cruz harbor. We were lucky to get away."

"How'd you manage that? If you don't mind my asking?" Jack didn't actually care. He was stalling and remembered that LeBoux liked to talk.

"I guess we can thank you for that. If you hadn't made Billy and I think the ship was going to blow up, we wouldn't have swum so far away from it." At that moment LeBoux's first mate, Billy, let his Winchester drop to his side and left his position behind the rock behind his boss and came forward. He had also dispensed with most of the sailor duds. Still, he was dressed in blue. Indigo suspenders went over his navy-colored wool shirt, connecting to denim pants, while retaining his sailor's cap. Never a man of many words, he gave Jack a cold glare, then looked to LeBoux, who continued. "When we saw the police come and board the ship, we knew we couldn't go back. Then we had to swim far enough from the ship to get ashore without them spotting us. Later, we found out the police seized the guns, the ship, and most of my crew."

"But how'd you get away?"

"Billy, here, knew someone on a ship heading north. We were able to work off our passage."

Jack had read the captain right—he liked to talk. Even to someone he hated. But the stall had done little to improve their circumstances. There were simply too many guns from too many directions, and Jack had none. He had but one card to play: LeBoux's greed. And that had to be why LeBoux had gone to so much trouble to lure him to this spot. "So, what do you want?" Jack had a pretty good idea.

"Why the golden sun of course. You took it from me; now I want it back."

"What if I don't have it?" And he didn't.

"Sure you do. And if you don't, it doesn't matter. I still want it. And you're going to get it for me. It's either the golden sun you took from me, or ten thousand in gold. That's what I figure it's worth."

"And why would I do that?" He knew, but tried not to show it.

The captain nearly laughed. "Because I have what you want above all else. And don't pretend that you don't know what I mean."

Jack found himself looking into Fawn's frightened eyes, then over to his nervous partner.

"That's right, cowboy. You'll do anything I want and you know it."

"How much time do I have?"

"You'll bring me the gold tomorrow or the girl and your friend are dead."

Jack shook his head. "Two days, any less is impossible. And I need Dan and our guns."

"You're not getting any guns, and your partner stays."

"Well, I can't do it without him." Jack was bargaining, but he would need every bit of help he could get.

LeBoux simply shook his head.

Jack leaned back in his saddle and crossed his arms. "Then you might as well shoot us all right now."

Dan's and Fawn's eyes grew very wide. They couldn't know that Jack was down to playing his last card, and it wasn't much. He needed Dan. Jack was banking on the captain's greed. LeBoux didn't create such an elaborate scheme just to kill him, although he surely had plans to do just that after he got the gold.

LeBoux was stewing over the ultimatum, Jack could see it plainly in his eyes. Two hostages were much better than one. And he didn't like conceding anything to a man like Diamondback McCall.

LeBoux then looked to his first mate. He returned a firm shake of the head.

Meanwhile, Jack remained in the saddle, as though resigned to his fate.

Finally, the captain announced, "All right, cowboy." He pointed back in the direction from which they came. "I'm going to send a rider to the top of that hill. Then you head back north. When he signals me that you're far enough from here, I'll let your friend go. While you're going north, we'll be taking the girl in another direction. If we see so much as a dust trail, she's dead."

"You hurt her and you'll all be dead!" Jack didn't make idle threats.

"Spare me the tough talk, cowboy. Be back here an hour after sunup in two days with my gold. If you're late, you'll never see her again!"

Chapter Seven

Banditos

LeBoux sent his man riding up the hill as planned. A while later, Jack was alowed to head north. He had no thoughts of going back. Not yet. The captain commanded a veritable fortress in that rocky pass. For the moment he would have to play LeBoux's game. Once he had what the pirate wanted, he'd at least have something to bargain with. A plan was forming in his mind, but it had more holes than one of his old targets. He would have to make it up as he went along. Simple as that.

He rode until he was out of sight of LeBoux's man on the hill, then waited. A half hour passed before Dakota reached him. Dan came up on his left and let out a long sigh. "This is a tough one, partner. Got any ideas?"

As they nudged their ponies into a trot, Jack stretched back for his saddlebag. After pulling the leather tie loose, he reached in and retrieved the revolver he had liberated from the gunslinger in Tucson. "Well, I think we're gonna need more of these." He slid the pistol behind his belt, by the buckle. "And we've got to get our hands on a lot of gold."

"How you figure on doin' that?"

"I don't really want to hold up a bank but I'm gonna do whatever it takes."

Dan nodded. "I overheard some of those scallywags braggin' after you left. They talked real loose, soon as you got out of sight. So, I did me some listenin'. It seems the captain found out you frequented these parts, and put out the word that he'd pay plenty for any information about you."

"But how could he beat us down there and set us up?"

"He was already there. I got the notion he's wanted in Arizona and doesn't dare cross the border. I bet he did some stealin' to finance his plan to get the gold sun back."

"So, we came his way and made it easy for him."

"Yup. That dude from the cafe heard us talkin' about riding down to Nogales. So he beat it down there to collect his reward. I got a hunch LeBoux had to cut him in on the deal, though. He doesn't strike me as an easy fella to do business with. The same's probably true for that hombre from the jail. Then they just had to pay off one of the Federales to put him in that cell, and the trap was set."

"I figured it had to be something like that. But I sure feel dumb for being suckered that way."

"Heck, partner. None of us saw it comin'."

Jack shook his head and they rode on. He weighed his options. There weren't many. There also wasn't much time, so he doubted there'd be a second chance. He was leaning toward a long shot partly because that was his nature, but also because he didn't think Fawn would approve of him robbing a bank.

His thoughts were suddenly interrupted when he noticed a dust trail comming their way. They were still at least a half dozen miles from the border and the four men riding fast toward them were definitely Mexicanos. Jack and Dan continued to head north. They were short on time and couldn't waste it. The opposing riders closed quicky, and then all pulled up short, stopping a dozen feet apart.

The Mexicanos were heavily armed. Cartridge belts crisscrossed their chests. Pistols loomed in double holsters and were also tucked in their waists. Winchesters lay across the top of each man's thighs and Jack noted that they even carried knives in sheaths attached to their boots.

Jack continued to hold the reins with his left hand, his right rested open on his thigh, in close proximity to the handle of the pistol. The four caballeros all had their hands gripped about their rifles' stock, with fingers inside the trigger guard. They were ready for a fight and so was Jack. They were obviously bandits and he'd have to make a stand.

The exploits of the marauding bandits along the border were well known. They had rampaged through the region for years, robbing and killing luckless travelers with impunity.

The man second to Jack's right was the biggest hombre. He was also a few years older than his amigos. It had been at least a week since any of them had had a bath and shave. The substantial layer of dust covering every inch of them indicated that they lived on the trail. That big hombre had a commanding presence and Jack was certain he was the leader. He had been giving the two men traveling north a careful study and a smile began to spread across his face, displaying a total of five yellow teeth. Noting the six-gun tucked in Jack's waist, he gave a quick chuckle. "The gringo's got a *pistola*." His accent was thick and he apparently spoke in English for the benefit of the Americanos. He then repeated it in Español with a glance to his muchachos.

They returned the laugh and didn't seem to perceive Jack as a particular threat to them. They held their Winchesters at the ready, but not right at him. These men were very proud and extremely confident.

The big man lost the smile and stared hard at Jack. "I want the *pistola*, gringo."

Jack stared back. "Why don't I give you what's inside of it, instead?"

A startled expression swept his unkempt face. "I

think you must be loco, gringo. Your amigo is unarmed, so it's four to one. Don't those numbers mean anything to you?"

"Yeah. It means I've got two more bullets than I need."

The big hombre pulled his head back a little and continued the stare. Then the corners of his mouth curled up slightly. "My name is Jose Luis Cardoza." His face did little to betray his pride.

Jack had heard of him. A man known for his ability with weapons and a propensity for using them often and harshly.

"Does that name mean anything to you, gringo?"

Jack returned a single nod. "Yeah. It means I'm gonna shoot you first."

Anger quickly consumed the proud bandito. Jack saw his grip around the rifle tighten and then all four hombres swung the barrels of their Winchesters toward him. The banditos had the advantage. They merely had to turn their weapons and fire. Jack had to reach, draw and hit four men. It happened in an instant.

Jack went for the revolver. The four opposing rifles came around to aim point-blank at the same time. Jack had to fan the hammer with his left hand. The Mexicanos merely had to squeeze their triggers. Four shots rang out in one continuous roar. The slugs hit home with lethal effect, stopping the battle as quickly as it had begun.

The bandits were very fast with their rifles. Jack was barely faster. With the smoke from Jack's revolver still hanging in the air, three of the four bandits instantly slumped over in different directions, and then two fell to the ground. Jack had just managed to hit each man in the chest before they had done the same to him. But Señor Cardoza was one tough hombre. As his rifle slipped from his grip, he glanced down at his fatal wound, put his left hand over the seeping bullet hole and looked up again. Pain and shock swept across his hard, dark features, as he gave Jack a bewildered stare. "You had no chance!" His voice was harsh and labored.

"I had no choice." Jack slid his pistol back behind his belt.

The light seemed to be dimming in Cardoza's eyes. Still, there seemed to be one more question in his eyes as he stared at Jack. "Who are you, gringo?"

"The name's McCall."

For the briefest of moments Jack noted a glint of recognition in the bandit's dimming eyes and then, they went dark. Five seconds later, he fell forward in the saddle, dead.

It was over, and a mighty close call. Far closer than Jack would have liked. Closer than any other fight he'd been in before. Desperately close to killing Jack and preventing him from saving Fawn, and he knew it.

With the battle over, it was time to gather the spoils of war.

Killing for Jack was always a sad and dismal business. No matter that the men he had just killed were killers themselves, he was the one that had killed them and he didn't like it one bit. The faces of four more men to haunt him during the dark dreams or sleepless nights. But at least this time their deaths served an immediate purpose. There was little doubt that he and Dan would need weapons in their efforts to save Fawn, and these four were bristling with guns, knives, and ammunition.

After taking what they needed, they laid the bodies of the four banditos over their saddles, tied them down, and gave the horses a slap across the flank. There was no time for burial. The horses would take them back to wherever they had come from. Someone would tend to it.

With enough weapons and ammunition for a small war, Jack and Dan headed north.

Chapter Eight

Ransom

The afternoon sun was settling in the western sky. A couple of more hours and it would start disappearing behind the hills. With its retreat, the temperature dipped. Not wanting to unnecessarily tire the horses, Jack and Dan had let them slow to a brisk walk. Over an hour had passed since the two men had crossed the border. Both men had plenty to think about, but not a single word had been spoken. Dakota finally broke the silence. "You sure the only way to deal with that pirate is to give him what he wants?"

"He's holding all the cards right now. I can't go charging in against all those guns when they're holding Fawn. And I don't even know where they took her. When we come back he's still gonna be hunkered down in that rocky fortress."

"What if I could get you in the back door of that fortress?"

Jack just gave him an inquiring look.

"Well, I tried my hand at prospectin' a few years back. Never found enough color in these hills to mention, but I ended up doing a little diggin' atop that mountain." He pointed back at Patagonia Mountain. "Anyway, there's an old miner up there named Dutch van Doer. He don't care much for most people, but we got along all right."

Jack wondered where Dan was going with the story but just let him talk.

"When I finally gave up on all the diggin' and pannin', he showed me the trail he found to get down that steep southern slope. That's how he got supplies. He'd take that steep trail down to the road to Nogales. It would put you a mile or so behind LeBoux and his men, and they wouldn't know how you got there. Not many folks know about it."

"That would be a reasonable gamble, ordinarily."

"Except their holdin' Fawn, and you won't chance it."

"I'm afraid he's got to at least think we're playing his game. If we've got what he wants we might have some leverage."

"Sounds like LeBoux's got the leverage. He probably knows the Federales aren't about to help us and the US authorities can't cross the border."

"And that leaves us paying his price."

"Well, partner, I don't see how you can do it. The banks don't keep that much gold on hand. They ship their gold and silver to the San Francisco mint regularly by train. And it's well guarded."

"How much gold is on those trains?"

"Don't know, Jack. But not ten thousand dollars worth. It's mostly silver they take out of the hills around here. And how would you know when they were gonna put it on that train?"

He didn't answer right away. "Maybe there's another way."

"I'm listenin', partner."

"What about the Apache gold in that canyon."

Dan gave a long stare. "That's a legend. Probably nothin' to it."

"Fawn put some stock in it." He turned to receive a look of skepticism. "You got a better idea?"

After a minute's thought, Dan shook his head.

"Then we better kick east. We've got to head back to the village and see the chief. I never got a close look at that sword."

It wasn't long before there was but a purple glow behind them, and it soon dimmed to gray. Then the night descended into an inky darkness. With it came the chill night air. The dimness proved a more difficult obstacle for the men than their horses and they ended up letting the animals find the way to the Anasazi village, which had become home to them.

It wasn't much past midnight when they reached the canyon city's entrance. Ten minutes later, they were climbing down the two long ladders, having already bedded their horses in the small stable.

It was, of course, midday for the Anasazi. The huge cavern was aglow from cooking fires and torchlights. A light of warm radiance. Red and orange hues lit the courtyard. Darker, scarlet shades reflected off the stone and masonry structures built high along the cavern walls. It cast a charm upon the village.

The tranquil atmosphere was an equal part of its charm. As they headed toward the chief's dwelling, Jack was struck by the many smiles he encountered. It then occurred to him that in all the time he had spent among these people he had never witnessed a dispute, let alone a physical altercation. Quite a contrast to the sort of violence he'd run into over the last few days in the world above.

As Jack and Dan made their way across the courtyard, they were met by Chota. He came from that darker part of the cavern, where the chief resided. It seemed that the sensitive man could read the worry in Jack's face that he was trying to hide. "You have problem, Jack?"

He saw no purpose in telling of Fawn's circumstance and didn't answer the question. "Can we see the chief?"

Chota's eyes narrowed, but he then simply turned for Tecanay's quarters, with Jack and Dan close behind. Once they reached the chief's lower-level dwelling, Chota quickly went inside while Jack and Dan waited by the doorway.

A minute later they were allowed to enter. They were welcomed by a wave of the hand and a concerned expression on the chief's face. There were the same mats positioned before him as their previous visit. Tecanay could read the worry in Jack's eyes. After a moment, he gestured for him to speak.

Chota was positioned beside the two men to translate. Jack simply asked, "May I take a close look at that sword?"

The chief was clearly puzzled by the request, but after another moment or two he reached around for the ancient weapon. He passed it to his guest without comment.

It wasn't the blade that drew his attention but the sheath. A simple dark leather scabbard graced with a silver tip. Someone, probably that conquistador, had used a sharp object to write an account of their quest for the Apache gold. Jack knew enough Spanish to understand the short text. It seemed that the soldiers had been told the tale from the chief of one of the northern tribes and warned of the dangers. Then it described the route they had used to find the canyon, including a small, and very crude, map.

While Jack memorized the landmarks along the route to the Apache canyon, he glanced up and noted the chief's questioning expression. The questions were never asked, however, and after Jack returned the sword to Chief Tecanay, they parted cordially.

It was an awkward business. Being secretive to people

that you respect and are fond of is distasteful. Yet Jack felt they were better off not knowing.

Although the cavern city was only halfway through its day, Jack and Dan went straight for their quarters to get some rest. It wasn't just the sounds, smells and light that made sleeping tough. As Jack closed his eyes, Fawn's frightened face would be there. When he'd try to focus on a plan, he wouldn't get very far with it. He simply had no idea of what he was facing. Could he even find the canyon described on that sword? Would he have to do as Dan suggested? Come charging in the back way. Of course he preferred to be able to deal with LeBoux. At least until he got Fawn free of him. Few minutes of sleep came to him, even fewer conclusions.

Soon the fires would be extinguished, signaling the end of the day for the Anasazi. Jack and Dan arose just a couple of hours before sunup. Chota had left two bowls of beans, tortillas and corn by the doorway. It seemed he expected them to be leaving and chose to forgo good-byes.

Less than an hour later they were leading their horses out of the boxed canyon. By the time they got out to the open desert, the first glow of morning appeared atop the mountains behind them.

Chapter Nine

Canyon of Gold

Daybreak came an hour after they turned south. They braced against another cold morning made worse by the accompanying breeze. The two men had been quiet, not a dozen words uttered between them. Of course it made sense, they had plenty on their minds.

Dan had been riding close at Jack's side. After a while Jack noticed his partner looking toward him. His mouth was in something of a twist, his eyes narrowed to slits. Jack turned to his friend. "What's on your mind, Dan?"

He began with some hesitation. "What do you figure the odds are of findin' this canyon?"

Jack looked ahead, obviously not caring for the question. "The odds are thin, too thin. We both know that."

"So, why you so bent on doin' it this way?"

"Because if I have what LeBoux wants, I can probably do some trading. No matter how unlikely this Devil's Canyon might seem, Dakota, I've got to at least try and find it. We've got a lot better chance of saving Fawn if we're holding gold. The idea is, to trade for her life."

"You think LeBoux's gonna go for that?"

"Why not? He gets what he wants most, me and the treasure."

"That's not much of a bargain, Jack. He's gonna kill you for sure and for spite!"

"It's a bargain I'm willing to make, if it comes to that." He added a single nod. "Just so long as Fawn's safe."

Dan's mouth returned to a twist. "That's your only plan?"

"No. I've got other plans."

"Are they any good?"

He shook his head. "Some are just worse than others."

"In that case, I guess I don't want to hear about 'em."

Jack managed a little smile and they rode on quietly for a couple of more hours. The sun continued to rise over the Santa Rita Mountain Range as they continued south. They were practically retracing the route they'd traveled the day before. Jack's mind was on Fawn and that map. He would do anything to protect her, but if she wasn't being held captive by those pirates he wouldn't be thinking in such defensive terms. Taking on that many guns was not beyond him. He had a coolness during gunplay that could narrow long odds. Even in the brief time that LeBoux's men showed themselves,

Jack had sized them up. It was an instinctive call. He could tell which men were a threat with a gun and which ones weren't. Knowing who to kill first could be very useful in the sudden-death moves of a gunfight. He wondered if it would end up that way. If he couldn't find the canyon of gold, it probably would. He looked ahead at the wide expanse of arid landscape and saw nothing like what was described on that soldier's map. The gently rolling desert plain stretched out before them, flanked by the foothills and mountains to their left and the Santa Cruz River several miles to their right. The breeze was traveling with them, warmed a little by the climbing sun.

Time ticked by with each man pondering their chances. When Jack said the odds were thin, that was no understatement. He was counting on the conquistador's description being somewhat accurate and that the canyon was within a day's ride. Since the Anasazi found the Spanish soldier within the hunting area of their village, that seemed quite possible. When he first saw the description on the sword's scabbard he realized that he had a more difficult problem. The conquistador's account clearly showed a mountain range and a river. Those were obviously the Santa Rita Mountains and the Santa Cruz River. They ran roughly parallel, north and south, for around fifty miles. Whether to go north or south was the question. It was really hard to figure since the map and description were rather vague. He finally made the decision to go south based on a simple fact. If it was north, it was simply too far. It wasn't likely that they could make it back across the border in time to make LeBoux's deadline if they had to start looking in the wrong direction. His decision was predicated more on hope than logic. So, Jack knew full well just how thin the odds were. They had one day to find a canyon that might be nothing but a legend and he didn't even know if they were going in the right direction.

Time and miles passed without seeing a single one of the symbols from the map. Jack was doubting the whole venture. He should have seen three pointed hills or rocks in a row by then. After that, the map indicated the mountain, to their left, with the word "acantilado," which means cliff, followed with an arrow symbol. In desperation, Jack found himself mulling over other plans. They were all variations of rapid-fire death, while trying to save Fawn in the process. Reckless plans of last resort. His heart sunk. The thought of losing her was unacceptable and he pushed those thoughts aside.

Twenty minutes later his eyes were drawn to the left. In the foothills, atop a flat bluff, were three pointed red rocks. They weren't particularly prominent points. In fact, Jack didn't notice them the previous day and he rode within half a mile of them. Still, he began to have just a little hope. They were the first features that resembled the description on the scabbard.

Jack turned his pony east toward the three points and Dan sided him. They were riding up into the foothills, heading almost straight for the mountain range. Soon, they were well above the cactus-strewn plain and into the ever thicker sagebrush. Another twenty minutes passed and the three rock points were behind. As Jack began looking toward the mountainside, Dan turned his way. "So, what are we lookin' for exactly, partner?"

"Best I can figure, Dan, there should be some sheer cliffs coming up. Then the entrance to the canyon."

"Jack, I've been riding all around these parts for years. Now, sure there's some pretty steep cliffs about a mile or so ahead, but there ain't no canyon. I'd have seen it. Heck, I did me some prospecting along here not more than a couple of years ago." He shook his head. "Think I'd notice a canyon if it was here."

"Yeah, I'm sure you're right. But I'd still like to take a look, if you don't mind?"

Dan shrugged and they rode on. The red cliffs appeared after a little while and Jack gave them a hard study. The red rock cliff went straight up, towering above the riders. A rugged mass of copper-colored stone. It looked as though a huge chunk of rock had simply been chiseled away from the the rest of the mountain, leaving this long wall of stone. The area of cliff spanned at least a quarter mile and the two soon rode passed it.

Jack looked ahead and then back. There was no sign of cliffs ahead. He looked to Dan. "Is that it? There's no more cliffs?"

"That's all there is, partner. Told you there ain't no canyon."

Jack wheeled his horse around. "We're going back."

Dan turned too. "How come?"

"I don't know. Maybe we missed something."

Dan let out a little sigh, but said nothing. They rode slowly, with Jack stopping occasionally for a more careful look. The cliff was no more than a hundred feet from them and Dan was puzzled by his partner's thorough scrutiny of what was obvious. It was just a wall of rock. Then, when they were about midway along the area of cliff face, Jack suddenly stopped again. He spun Chilco around and glanced over to Dan. "Did you see that?"

"See what?"

"A shadow."

Dan returned another shrug and a mystified expression.

Jack gave a quick tilt of the head toward a thin dark area in the rock face, and nudged his mount right for the cliff. Dan reluctantly followed, but stayed back some, maybe forty feet behind. He watched his partner ride toward the red wall as though he would ride right into it. Then, just before contacting the stone face, Jack turned his pony left and disappeared into an unseen space in the rock.

Dan's eyes grew wide and his head drew back in disbelief. Within seconds he reached the wall and saw the tight slit. It couldn't be seen unless you were right next to it. Even then you couldn't tell that it was a passage that went deeper. Because the passage veered left and right, it simply appeared as lighter and darker shades of rock. They rode into the zigzag passageway until it finally widened enough for two horses to stand side by side about fifty feet in. By the time Dan reached that wide spot, Jack was already standing ahead of his horse, holding the reins, and peering around the corner. At that point, the narrow passage stopped and the canyon lay before them.

Dan dismounted, led his mount alongside Chilco, and cautiously came up close behind Jack. He spoke at a whisper. "I've been wrong before, partner, but I'd have bet my last dollar this wasn't here."

Jack kept looking out into the narrow canyon. "I've got to admit, I didn't hold much hope of it being here either, Dakota." He glanced back at his partner. "I guess sometimes you have to go for the longshot."

Dan nodded. "So, what's out there?"

"It's a pretty tight canyon, goes in around a quarter mile, then stops. The walls on both sides go straight up for close to a hundred feet, then terrace up into the mountain slopes. Even from on top of the two mountain tops, you couldn't see the canyon."

"Any sign of Apaches, or gold?"

"Looks like the entrance to a mine, maybe a couple hundred yards on the right. Just past that, there's a corral with close to forty ponies, Apache ponies. There're also mounds of rock and dirt along most of the canyon on the left side and more down at the end."

"How many Apaches?"

"Hard to say. I saw three men going into the mine and there're a couple dozen huts past the corral." Jack took another scan of the canyon, then turned to Dan. "I've got a feeling there're more than enough Indians to go around. I'll have to wait for dark before going in."

Dan swallowed before answering. "What's my part in this, Jack?"

"Your part comes a mite later."

"Sounds like you've got a plan."

"Maybe. Right now we've got to find a place to hide. It won't be dark for a couple more hours."

Chapter Ten

Glory Hole

They found a wash deep enough to conceal the horses and themselves a few hundred yards down the foothills. When darkness arrived, Jack readied to slip into the canyon. Dan was left with simple instructions. Stand by and stay alert. He would hold both horses within the wash, saddled and ready to go.

Jack moved out quietly and was soon back to the end of the passageway. His spurs were left behind to avoid noise. He also carried Dan's saddlebags to, hopefully, hold the gold. He carefully looked around the edge of the rock where it opened to the narrow canyon, but couldn't see far. It was a dark, moonless night, with only starlight and a faint orange glow from the mine entrance piercing the dim gorge. The canyon was also very quiet. Only a distant pinging which seemed to be coming from within the mine. It was a muffled, metallic sound, barely audible from where Jack stood.

He saw no guards and figured it would be fairly easy to get to the mine, his presence masked by the minimal light. With stealth and caution, he started to slowly make his way into the canyon. But after only a few steps, he abruptly stopped and became as rigid as the stone wall beside him. It was a noise that suddenly came echoing through the brisk night air that stopped him cold. He stood and listened. There was a brief silence, and then the unwelcome sound of voices that seemed to be coming from the huts beyond the corral. Jack slowly made his way back into the passageway and once again, peered around the edge of the rock. Within minutes, campfires began to appear in the hut area and Jack could then see that part of the canyon clearly. Over the next half hour he counted twenty-three men around the huts. He also noted several going in and out of the mine.

Occasionally, there would be a lull in the voices and he could, momentarily, hear the pinging sound again. He stayed there, watching, for over four hours.

It wasn't long after the last fire was extinguished that the voices also became mute. There was still the occasional pinging sound, but it seemed that sleep had descended on the area outside the mine.

Jack quietly began moving toward the mine, staying close to the vertical wall on the right side of the canyon so he could blend into the dark shadows if necessary. Ten minutes later, he stood at the entrance to the mine, and listened. There was still that metallic tapping and he recognized the sound. It sounded like one man using a hammer. He heard nothing else. There was a glow from within the mine, and that was the risky part, yet he reasoned if someone was working with a hammer, they wouldn't be watching the entrance.

Jack peered around the edge. He had been in enough mines to know what he was looking at. Over the centuries, the Apaches had been following a vein of gold. Starting at the base of the canyon, it went into the side of the mountain, and then straight down. It seemed that they had found the mother lode, for the shaft grew larger twenty feet inside and then opened up to a huge pit. There was a flat walkway, six to eight foot wide, surrounding the pit. On the far side of the pit were a couple of dark shafts. Jack figured they were abandoned attempts to follow the gold vein, before they started digging downward.

The sound and light emanated from deep within the abyss, in what miners call a glory hole. Jack carefully approached the sixty-foot opening of the chasm, then got to his knees and looked down. It was a vast vertical shaft, at least a couple of hundred feet deep. A working gold mine, with ropes and large animal-skin bags for bringing up the rock. The ropes were tied to poles above the pit. The poles rested in holes cut into the rock floor. Jack wondered which was the tougher job, digging out the rock, or pulling it up from on top. Then he noted the long rope ladder used to reach the bottom of the mine. He couldn't help but admire the physical ability of the men at the bottom. It was a long way up, after digging rock all day.

There was also a furnace for doing metalwork at the bottom. It was a simple round brick hearth, with three leather bellows placed around it to raise the heat of the coals.

But it was more than just a mine. It was a holy place, a shrine. Spaced evenly in a spiral pattern were a series of ledges jutting out from the walls of the circular pit. A total of thirteen stone platforms graced the mine shaft, each one about four foot square. Standing on all but the last, deepest platform, were giant statues. Half the figures were tall bird and flying serpent creatures. They were interspersed with equally large statues of warriors. They were surely representations of gods, and the great deities seemed to be watching over the mere mortals that worked below them. They were close to fifteen feet tall and all made of shimmering gold. Rugged metal figures made of a patchwork of gold plate.

It seemed that the one man who remained in the pit was the metalworker. Jack watched him at his craft. It was a long way down, but he could see him clear enough, the glowing coals casting a warm amber hue around the worker. He was shirtless, understandable from his proximity to the furnace, and his bare skin glistened from sweat.

The procedure was simple. Place gold nuggets in among the coals with two stone spoons, work the bellows to bring up the heat, then retrieve the hot metal and place it on a flat rock. He would then begin pounding the nuggets flat with a stone hammer. After that, he'd heat up the plates again, then hammer them against variously shaped stones to form them. When he finally got them sculpted to the desired shape, he would then fasten them to other plates. The attachment was a strange process of grinding small holes with a sharp stone, then tapping in small golden tacks.

It was a crude method of metal art, but impressive considering what the Apache had to work with. It was also tediously slow. The Indians probably didn't mind the length of time it took to do small amounts of work, since it was a labor for the gods. Jack, however, was running out of time. He had watched the metal worker for hours and was beginning to wonder if he would ever call it a night.

With no more than an hour before first light, the metalworker headed for the long rope ladder. Jack went around to the first of the dark shafts behind the pit and stood a few feet inside. He was completely concealed in inky blackness. But the time it took for the worker to climb was starting to make Jack uncomfortable. It would be light very soon and the Apache miners could return at any moment. It wasn't a good place to be discovered, with only one way out, and the Apache cavalry just outside the door. Still, he had made his play, and would just have to wait it out.

Twelve long minutes ticked by as the metalworker

inched his way up. Jack spent that time watching the mine entrance and listening for any sign of life from the canyon. All seemed quiet, other than the labored breathing of the worker as he got close to the top.

Once he reached the last rungs and pushed himself up onto the walkway with his hands, he let out a heavy sigh, and rose to his feet. He slowly walked out of the mine; then Jack dashed for the nearest rope hanging over the side. The rope was intended to haul up rock from the bottom. Jack used it for a fast descent. He grabbed the rope, let himself down a little, and then twirled the roped between his legs and boots to control the speed. He reached the bottom in seconds.

The embers inside the furnace still burned dimly, giving off enough light to see around. Jack gave but token notice to the primitive equipment used to extract the rock and ore. Various shaped stone implements attached to stout wooden handles by leather straps stood leaning against one wall. There were also stone wedges and sharp flints used to drive between the rocks to loosen them. They were laying close by the other tools.

Also of little interest to him were the beginnings of another statue. Behind the furnace were the nearly completed legs of another warrior. They stood side by side, the uppermost plates still warm from being in the hearth that very evening. Jack had watched the metal worker using the gold tacks to affix the newly formed metal just before he left the mine. Like most construction, it was done from the ground up.

What did attract Jack's attention was a mound of gold nuggets close to the furnace. Hundreds of pounds of gold in all sizes and shapes in a large heap. The value of so much gold was beyond his speculation, but certainly sufficient to make a person quite rich. Yet he felt most uncomfortable as he filled his saddlebags with the precious metal. Honor was as much a part of him as was his love for Fawn. And although he knew what he was doing was necessary, he also knew it was wrong. There was no excuse for thievery, plain and simple. The code of the West was strict and he had lived by it all his life. He had never broken it before and didn't like the way it made him feel. He made up his mind, right then, that no matter the risk, he'd bring the gold back. All of it. With that pledge made, he finished filling the two saddlebags, and went for the rope ladder.

The weight of the gold hanging over his shoulder made the long climb feel even tougher. But he knew time wasn't on his side and first light would make its presence known very soon. He climbed fast, reaching the top in little more than a minute. Then, with his heart pumping hard from the effort and his breath louder than he would have liked, he looked over the edge. No one was yet in the mine, but he could hear voices outside.

Within seconds, Jack was at the mine entrance, and peering in the direction of the huts. Fires were being lit and at the very same instant, the sky to the east was just starting to glow. At that moment, the men by the huts were occupying themselves with the fires and the canyon was still quite dark. That wouldn't last for long. Jack made his way along the canyon wall, while keeping an eye on the huts. In a handful of minutes, he was back in the safety of the narrow passage. He took one more look and knew he had not been spotted.

By the time he was through the passage, the desert plain was coming to light, but an idea was coming to light too. He gave a couple of whistles to Dan, a pre-arranged signal, and turned back for the passageway. While Dan was bringing the horses up, Jack went back to where the passage met the canyon. There was enough light by then to easily see the huts. They could see him too. Jack pulled out his left revolver and fired it three times in the air. He stood there long enough so that the Apaches got a good look at him, and then quickly made for Dan and the horses.

Chapter Eleven

The Cavalry

Jack came out of the passageway at a dead run. Dan had the horses twenty feet from the entrance. He sat aboard his mount and was holding Jack's stallion by the bridle. Jack stopped just long enough to affix the saddlebags to the rear of his saddle before swinging up onto Chilco. He dug his heels into the stallion's flanks and Dan did the same to his pony. Both horses were at a full gallop in five jumps. Dan had to yell over the driving hooves and snorting nostrils. "What was that shootin' back there, partner?"

"Thought maybe we'd need some help! I called in the cavalry!"

"Are you talkin' about the Apaches?"

"No better fighters on horseback in the world than the Apache," Jack yelled while looking over his shoulder.

He noted that none of the warriors had come through the passageway.

"You put those Indians after us on purpose?" Dan called out as he also took a glance back.

"Yeah. At this point, I'll take what I can get."

Dan's expression showed extreme disapproval. It wasn't like Dan to doubt Jack, but at that moment, he surely did. The wisdom of deliberately bringing a band of angry Apaches down on them eluded him. It seemed worse than risky, it seemed dumb. The Apaches weren't just fearless fighters, they were blood-thirsty and cruel. He had seen what they had done to their victims when he was a deputy. Torture and mutilation were standard practice and Dan was getting more than a bit worried.

Jack had, of course, measured the risks. And it wasn't that he thought it was a particularly good plan, just better than anything else. He was counting on being able to put some distance between themselves and the pursuers. The Apache, in spite of being great warriors, had some catching up to do. Jack and Dan were racing across the desert while the Indians were scrambling to grab their weapons and get all those horses out of the corral at once. Jack also knew that passageway allowed but one horse at a time. He was hoping for a few minutes' delay before the whole force of forty-some braves gave chase.

Jack figured four minutes, but the Apaches were better than that. Barely three minutes ticked by before they took up the pursuit. That still put more than a mile between hunter and quarry, but Jack needed more time.

Up until then, as they charged in the direction of LeBoux and his gang of thieves, the captain had held all the cards. Jack had one bet left. He was about to raise the stakes in a most dangerous game, but he needed a minute or two, and a poker face, in order to play out the hand. The Apaches were the wild card, but if Jack couldn't somehow gain a minute or two on the hostiles in pursuit, there would be no winners, except the Apaches.

Jack and Dan had managed to maintain their lead on the Indian cavalry as they finally got within the last few miles of the rocky canyon where LeBoux was waiting with his men and Fawn. Jack had deliberately headed a little west of their destination, so he could cut back east when they got into the rocks that could cover their turn.

The Apache were skilled trackers, so Jack couldn't expect to delay them for long. Jack's plan was going to come down to a handful of seconds and he was none too sure that it wouldn't end up bloody.

Ten minutes later, they were heading along the base of the tall hill that was no more than a mile from LeBoux's position. The captain had positioned one of his men atop the landmark to monitor Jack's and Dan's approach, to see that they came alone, and signal that information back to LeBoux. It was at that point that Jack told his partner the details of his plan and left Dan to stay about a quarter mile from where LeBoux and his thugs were waiting.

Seconds later, Jack pulled Chilco to a stop, five feet short of the captain and his men. They all gave Jack a hard stare, not appreciating the dust he brought with him. The twelve men were all mounted, as though they expected to conclude business quickly, and move on. Jack hoped so too. LeBoux was at the very front. The rest of his men were lined up on both sides of him. They all held rifles, or pistols, straight at him. Fawn was behind LeBoux. Her hands were tied before her and the reins of her horse were tied to the captain's saddle. LeBoux's face betrayed any attempt to disguise his anger and suspicion. His eyes were narrow and they flashed toward Dan, who still lingered near the large hill. "What's he waiting for?"

"He's just watching." Jack gestured toward his partner with a flick of his eyes. "He's watching to see how you're going to play this. He's also watching for the Apaches."

"What Apaches?" The suspicion was even more present in LeBoux's expression.

Jack noted LeBoux's lookout from atop the hill was at that moment racing down in their direction. "The Apaches your man spotted from up there." He pointed toward the lookout and added, "The Apaches that want their gold back." Jack reached back and grabbed the heavy saddlebags, then nudged his horse close enough to hand them over to the captain, who quickly checked the contents. Jack then looked hard into LeBoux's eyes, a cold, deadly serious glare, and added, "You've got the gold. Hand over the girl and we'll all live through this."

LeBoux's scout from on top of the hill came charging

in with a thick cloud of dust behind him. When he got within a hundred feet of his comrades, he yelled out with alarm, "Indians! There must be fifty of 'em!" He brought his horse to a stop and gave his boss an agitated glare.

Jack didn't even look the man's way. He just kept his stare locked on LeBoux. "We've only got a minute or two. They're trying to find their way here through the rocks. But you fire a shot and they'll be down on us like a swarm of angry hornets."

It seemed clear that the last thing the captain wanted was to let Jack get away again. Even with death coming at them like an express train, indecision engulfed him. Jack could read that in his face, as precious seconds slipped away. He pressed him harder. "Take the gold and run—if you try anything else I told Dan to start firing his rifle. It's real simple, LeBoux—you try to kill us, and we're taking the lot of you with us."

With time just about gone, Jack realized that the captain was nearly as scared of him as he was the Indians. Jack had to give him a dangerous concession or they'd all be dead. "All right LeBoux, you and your men go first, and we'll go the other way."

By that time, three of LeBoux's men had already lost their nerve and turned to leave the canyon. The other four were staring at the large dust cloud to the north. It rose above the large rocks, announcing the oncoming Apaches. They were so close that their horses' pounding hooves sounded like rumbling thunder.

LeBoux finally realized that he had no options and

even less time. After pulling the knot free releasing the reins of Fawn's horse, he spurred his mount back through the rocky canyon. The rest of his men had already done so, leaving with great haste. LeBoux followed on their heels.

Jack didn't have to signal Dan, who was coming in fast. He arrived just as Jack had cut Fawn's hands loose and given her the reins. They also headed out through the canyon, but would kick east as soon as possible. A mile ahead was the road to Nogales. LeBoux and company were driving hard for the border town. Jack could see them, a quarter mile in the distance. He could also see the Apache. They were even closer, a few hundred yards behind. Jack led them through the turn east and followed along the foothills that gradually rose to meet the steep slopes of Patagonia Mountain.

It was rocky country and they were using the rocks as cover whenever possible. Jack would cut around and between the huge boulders, trying to confuse the chasers and avoid giving them easy targets.

The Apaches were near enough to fire occasional shots and some of those bullets were coming too close for Dakota's liking. One creased his hat and that bothered him more than a little. The sporadic rounds whizzing by were unnerving, but as Jack glanced back he noted that there weren't quite as many giving chase. About half had peeled off to chase LeBoux. That left about twenty. Too many to take on, but he had another idea. Jack slowed his pony just enough to let Dan come up on his right. He yelled over, "Think you can find the trail up the mountain you told me about?"

"Sure, it ain't far."

"You said it was hidden behind some rocks?"

"Yup, big ones. You figure on duckin' in among them rocks, then headin' on up that mountain?"

"You got a better plan?"

"I ain't got a plan, but we gotta do somethin'."

Jack answered with a nod, then slowed again to pass the scheme on to Fawn. They rode tightly together, so when they moved, it would be as one.

Dan led the way, with the Apache just out of sight as they rounded a series of column-like gray rocks to their left. Then, with a suddenness, Dan pulled his mount back, and turned him hard left in between two particularly big rocks. It was all that Jack and Fawn could do to stay with him, nearly careening into his side as he made the desperate maneuver. The trail had come up on Dan a little sooner than expected, taking all by surprise. But with that nearly instantaneous move, they managed to disappear without the Apache seeing what happened. Within seconds, they were twenty-odd yards back within the cluster of huge stones. They quickly dismounted and followed Dan around a tall rock that nearly butted against the hillside. By the time the Apache reached that position, Dan, with Fawn and Jack close behind, were hidden.

Chapter Twelve

Trail of Blood

It didn't surprise Jack that few knew of the trail. Not only was the start of it difficult to find, it began as a series of steep switchbacks more suited to a mountain goat than man or horse. The narrow trail first angled back and forth behind the tall rocks. It was such a severe ascent that it was necessary to lead the horses up. In fact, it took quite a lot of coaxing to get the hesitant animals up the path. Once they got a little ways above the rocks the sheer gradient eased some. Dan led the climb with Jack at the rear. At that point they were going east, the same direction as the Apaches. Soon, the three climbers were about a hundred feet above the foothills, and Jack took a long sweeping scan of the terrain ahead. He could see the band of Indians a couple of miles ahead. They were stopped, having lost sight of their quarry in an area that was mostly flat, beyond the large rocks.

Jack and his fellow climbers were still leading their horses. The trail was dangerously sloped, with numerous broken patches. Jack took note of how the crumbling track continued east for another hundred yards before it finally switched sharply back west. The condition of the trail required a slow and cautious process and this gave Jack an uneasy feeling. He could see how the Apache were looking in all directions, trying to catch a glimpse of them. But it would take several minutes before the trail would veer back and take the three of them out of sight over a mountain crest. In the meantime, they were clearly silhouetted against the mountainside, and easily seen. He hoped the Apache wouldn't think to look up as high as they were, but doubted they'd be that lucky.

Jack kept an eye on the Apache force and saw them suddenly split up. About half of them continued east at a gallop. The rest headed back west to see if they could pick up a trail. There were eleven Indians in that group and they quickly fanned out so they could investigate a wider area, going in and around the rocks and gullies that made up that terrain. Then two of them suddenly cut north, back toward the mountain. In a matter of minutes they would reach the foothills where they'd have to turn west to follow along the mountain steps. Jack could see that it wouldn't be long before they'd be beneath them and he was getting anxious. It was a bad place to be discovered—no cover, on foot, and one false step could send one of them down onto the rocks.

The two Apaches rode at a trot and Jack calculated their speed and distance. He called out, "We've got to go faster, Dakota. Those Apache will pick us off with no trouble if we don't move it."

Dan hadn't even noticed the two braves coming in their direction. His attention had been entirely on the broken trail. When he spotted them, he gulped noticeably. "This ain't good, partner!" He tugged at his pony's reins and got more speed out of his own legs than Jack would have imagined. Jack and Fawn matched his nearly reckless pace and Dan quickly reached the switchback. That was also just about the time the two Apaches reached the foothills and made the turn west. Jack knew there could be no delay if there was to be any chance of eluding the two scouts.

The trail angled back at a steep angle and would quickly put Dan above Fawn and Jack. Dakota made his way around the tight bend, but his horse balked. It was a more difficult turn for creatures with four legs. Dakota took a few more steps up the trail, turned back so he faced the stubborn animal and pulled hard on the reins. This was no time to stop and Fawn did the only thing she could think of: give Dan's horse a slap across the left flank. The result was to cause the horse to bolt forward instantly and release the pressure on the reins. Dan, as a result, fell uncontrollably backward. He fell down hard, and immediately started to slide down the trail toward the oncoming hooves of his own horse. The startled horse stopped as Dan's left leg went between its front hooves. Then the momentum of the fall caused him to start sliding off the sloping trail. His right arm came off first, then his shoulder, and then he felt a grip on that right arm. Fawn had dropped her horse's reins and reached up with both hands to help her friend. She managed to momentarily stop him but it was a lot of weight for her and she couldn't hold him for long.

Jack was in a tough spot, behind Fawn's horse and too far away to help. There were only two options. To somehow get over or around her mount to reach Dan before he fell, and maybe take Fawn with him. Or toss them a line. The first notion was risky and would likely be too late. He spun around fast and reached back for the rope, which hung from his saddle horn. But before his hand quite touched the lasso, shots rang out!

The two Apache fired four times before Jack was able to answer. They were close to a hundred yards out and their aim was good. While the sound of the Apache's Winchesters cracked the air and the rounds whistled in and around the three floundering climbers, Jack responded with rapid fire from both his Colts.

The advantage was clearly with the Apaches. They held the long guns and not even Jack could be as accurate as a rifle at such a distance. Still, his .45-caliber slugs rained in so close that the two Indians felt the force of several bullets above their heads. Jack was able to force the scouts to dismount by sending twelve bullets their way in a matter of seconds. Then, in the moment it took for both Apache to jump off their mounts and duck into a crouch, Jack reached back and retrieved his own Winchester from his saddle.

As the bullets first arrived, Dan felt his back begin to slide off the trail and his weight buckled Fawn's arms. He had managed to hold on to the reins with his left hand, but there was too much slack to do him any good. Then, his left leg brushed against the inside of his horse's left leg. He instantly bent his knee around the animal's hoof, but he continued to fall. He was falling in an arch, caused by the pivot point of his leg wrapped about the horse's hoof. But he was also falling right on top of Fawn. In less than a second, she felt his full weight hit upon her shoulder, the blow driving her back, away from the hillside. She was reeling back, an instant from hurtling onto the rocks. In that last fleeting moment, she and Dan reached out for each other's hands. Dan stretched his right hand out for all he was worth, and grabbed hard around her wrist. She worked her fingers around his stubby wrist and they each felt the pull of her weight when his knee around the horse's ankle suddenly ended their descent. For a moment or two they swung back and forth. Dan hung there upside down, holding Fawn below him.

They were suspended high above the rocks below. Then, unexpectedly, the horse lifted its leg out of Dan's hold and they started down again. Dakota's feet came around at the same time the combined weight of him and Fawn hit home against his grip. His hand slipped several inches until it painfully reached the knot and their fall came to a stop.

His horse's head dropped low from the load, but it was a far more sustainable burden for his horse than it was for Dan's hand. They didn't have much time and Fawn knew it. She quickly made use of Dan's belt and loose clothes to pull and work her way up to the reins clinched in Dakota's grip. In a matter of seconds, she was pulling herself, hand over hand, up the leather straps until she could get a knee back onto the trail. She then braced herself, and began helping Dan back up to the trail. It was most difficult for her, however, between Dakota's weight and all the bullets flying around them.

Much of Dan's and Fawn's close call was unseen by Jack, not that he could have done anything about it. He had to keep his attention on the men shooting at them. It wasn't a position he liked, not being able to help the people he cared most about. But at least now that Jack held his rifle, the battle was a little more even. It was, of course, still two to one, but Jack's skill made up for much of that. There was another element of the skirmish that only Jack knew. The Apache clearly wanted their gold and probably more important to them, no witnesses to tell about their secret canyon. Jack, on the other hand, had no interest in killing the Apaches, only escaping from them. They were, after all, only protecting something that was sacred to them and trying to get back what was stolen from them. So, for the moment, he was putting his shots within inches of the feet of the two scouts. In response, they began to gradually back up, but they continued to fire.

Just at the time that Dan finally managed to pull himself up on the trail and back on his feet, the battle changed. Jack had just emptied his Winchester and had to reach back to his saddlebag to get more cartridges. That lull emboldened the Apache and they opened up on them. Shots rained in, and by the time Jack held the box of shells in his hand, he heard a low moan from just up the trail. He could just see around Fawn's horse. Dan had fallen to his knees and was clasping his left thigh with blood-soaked fingers.

Jack preferred not to kill the two scouts, but he had to stop them from firing. For the next few seconds there was quiet as both sides reloaded. Jack knew it would come down to who finished first and he took a calculated risk. He quickly slammed two rounds in, leveled the barrel, and took aim. Just as the two Apache slid the last cartridges in the receivers, Jack fired. With his usual precision, he put a slug in both men's right shoulders. Each one spun around from the impact and pain, dropping their rifles at their feet. They then quickly moved to their right for cover.

The two scouts, at least for the moment, were out of the fight as they tended to their wounds, but the respite would not last long. The brief battle had drawn the

attention of the other nine Apaches who had been trying to pick up the trail over the rock-strewn region.
They were coming to join the fight at a gallop. A few
more minutes and they'd be in rifle range.

Jack reloaded and called out with equal speed. "If we
don't make it over that crest before the rest of those
Apache get here, it's gonna get real bloody!"

Fawn wasted no time with words. She pulled Dan to
his feet, reached up, and gave his horse a hard slap. The
horse moved a couple of steps and she began pulling
Dan by the hand. Dakota was willing enough; it was
just that his leg was very painful. But between the two
of them, they got around the turn quickly, and Fawn
was soon coaxing Dan's horse up the steep grade by
continuing to strike its flank.

Jack used the same approach on Fawn's mount and
within a couple of minutes, they were all on the upper
trail and nearing the ridge. At that point the trail leveled
out, disappearing from sight on a flat plateau. Although
the climbers couldn't see it from where they were, the
trail would then lead them up to a rock bluff and a narrow pass.

The Apaches were coming fast but not as a single
group. They had been spread out along the rocky, rolling
landscape in an effort to find their quarry. The first rider
to get close enough to be a danger raised his rifle while
bearing down on the three climbers. Jack brought his
Winchester around at the same time and the two men exchanged fire. A single bullet grazed the brim of Jack's

black Stetson. He felt the wind and heard the snap from the round as it ripped through the air, three inches from his left ear. No one had ever come so close to ending his life before and he admired the man's skill. It was a remarkable shot considering that the Apache warrior made it while riding at full speed from a couple of hundred yards out. Jack's aim wasn't bad either. His shot hit the hard-charging Indian in the left forearm. The accompanying pain caused the man to drop his weapon and abandon the fight.

With that warrior turning away, there was a brief pause before the next three Apache riders got close enough. In those seconds, Fawn and Dan were able to climb over the crest before the bullets, once again, began to fly. It was a quick exchange of fire, with Jack directing his shots close around the heads of the advancing trio of hostiles while he also made his way up the steep path. He would fire two or three rounds and then move up the trail until he, too, was safely over the crest and out of the line of fire. The Apache bullets had all fallen short, none closer than a half-dozen yards from Jack's feet, so the last skirmish was a draw.

That was fine with Jack. He didn't blame the Apaches one bit and didn't feel particularly good over the outcome of the battle. Although no one was killed, four men were wounded. Dan had taken another bullet in the leg that was intended for him, but worst of all, he knew it wasn't over. Those Indians would find the trail, take up the chase, and press for a fight.

Chapter Thirteen

Narrow Escape

Once Jack and company were over the crest and momentarily safe, they stopped to tend to Dakota's leg. Jack and Fawn each took an arm, and eased him to the ground. Jack then used his knife to cut a few inches of the blood-soaked trousers to expose the seeping wound. It hit midway between the the knee and hip and fortunately missed the bone. The slug was still lodged in the fleshy part but was too deep to deal with on the trail.

There was nothing to do but stop the bleeding, so Jack went to his saddlebags for a suitable dressing. He hadn't used his city clothes for some time and didn't mind using the white shirt for a bandage and cutting his gray trousers into long strips to tie it in place. Dan hadn't said a word, but merely gritted his teeth, and tried not to look at his wound. He was pale and weak. He seemed content to just gaze at the mountain peaks above them. Then, while Jack and Fawn were busy putting the bandage in place, he looked to Jack and spoke almost apologetically. "Partner, I think I'm gettin' too old for this sort of thing."

"This isn't fun?" Jack asked without looking up from wrapping the last strip and tying it off. He hoped the sarcasm might bring back his partner's usual sense of humor.

Dakota twisted his mouth. "I gotta tell you, Jack, being chased by a passel of hostile Apaches ain't near as much fun as it used to be. And there's got to be a better way to see the view than hangin' upside down from a cliff. Tell you the truth, I don't enjoy gettin' shot much anymore, either."

They were finished patching up his leg, and Jack looked right into Dan's weary eyes. "Well, there's something else you're not gonna like."

Dan's eyes narrowed.

"It's not over. Those Apaches aren't about to give up. They're going to find the start of this trail before long and they'll be after us again for sure."

Dakota's expression changed very little. "You got a plan, partner? I mean, you've always got a plan."

"Well, I intend to see that no more bullets come at you two. If that's what you mean."

Fawn didn't like the way he said that and it showed in her tone. "You're not planning on sacrificing yourself for us, are you?"

"I wouldn't put it like that. But I figure I can hold them off for quite a while." He pointed toward the narrow split in the red rock butte, less than a quarter mile up the trail. "That's a mighty tight pass. Looks like no more than one at a time can get through. Once we get to the other side, I can keep them busy until the both of you are long gone."

"That sounds real noble but I don't like it. You just got finished saving me from those pirates, then I'm supposed to leave you to fight off all those Apaches by yourself?"

Dan was nodding with her last few words. "That goes for me too, partner. I might not be in the best of shape but I can still pull a trigger. And if you can hold them off at the other side of that butte, the three of us should be able to send 'em back down the mountain."

"I'm afraid nothing, short of killing them, is gonna stop those warriors. But I don't want any more bloodshed. The way I figure it, they're just trying to protect what's sacred to them." Jack gave a single nod. "With any luck, I can keep them bottled up long enough for you to get a safe distance away. Then I'll make a break for it."

Fawn's face clearly showed displeasure, but before she could speak, Dan motioned that he wanted to stand and she and Jack helped him to his feet. As soon as he steadied himself, he put his hand on Fawn's shoulder, turned her away from Jack, and motioned with his head for her to move ahead. They stopped a few steps away from his partner. Jack was left to watch, as Dan spent nearly half a minute whispering in her ear. Then they turned back to Jack, and Fawn spoke calmly. "All right, we'll do it your way. Now let's get going before it's too late."

Jack was surprised that she gave in so easily, but he knew she was right. They needed to get through that opening between the rocks before the Apaches showed up. Still, he wondered what Dan had said that changed her mind. But he wasn't about to ask. If she wanted him to know, she would have told him right off. She was fiercely independent, and not the least bit hesitant about playing things her way. Jack was simply glad they decided to play it safe, whatever the reason.

The trail had a fairly straight and gentle incline all the way up to where it reached a narrow split that divided the tall butte. Erosion over the centuries had left a nearly vertical clump of reddish brown rock resting at the peak of the slope. Were it not for the crack right through its center, Jack would see no way around it without great risk. On either side, the hillside had steep slopes and loose footing. And climbing the sixty-foot rock face was equally tricky. It was almost straight up. Yet he knew the tenacity of the men chasing them.

There was no longer a need to lead the horses. Jack helped Dakota up into the saddle; then when all three were on board, they nudged their mounts up the trail. Minutes later, they entered the narrow pass.

It was extremely close quarters, and Jack studied the

jagged rock walls that towered above them. The rock appeared to have simply split apart, leaving a three to four-foot-wide cut, straight through the giant rock. *Perhaps an ancient earthquake,* Jack thought, but whatever the geological cause, it gave Jack a tactical advantage.

A couple of minutes was all it took to reach the other side of the pass. From that point the trail leveled out briefly before heading back up the next hillside. It then weaved in and around scrub oaks and ponderosa pines that suddenly appeared in abundance with the higher altitude.

Jack dismounted, went to his saddlebags, and retrieved all the rifle ammunition he had commandeered from the banditos. He then tied his horse's reins around a heavy rock that kept the animal out of the range of fire.

Dan and Fawn were side by side a short distance up the fairly wide trail and looked back at his preparations. Fawn turned her horse around and nudged the animal close to him. "You sure they're still coming after us?"

Jack looked up to her and gave two slow nods. "Yeah, I can hear them; they're on the lower part of the trail. They'll be inside this pass in no more than five minutes. You two best make tracks." He said it matter-of-factly, displaying his customary and almost casual confidence.

She turned to Dan and then back to Jack. "So, how long do you plan on holding them off?" She didn't seem frightened, but certainly didn't share his confidence.

He glanced down the tight pass and looked back to

her with a slight smile. "This time I've got the advantage. I can keep them bottled up here for hours."

"All right. But just remember, they're good too. Be careful, sweetheart!"

Jack answered with a nod, and they headed up the trail. He was relieved that they didn't linger, since he hadn't told her everything. Although he was pretty sure that he could stop the Apaches from charging through the pass, he figured that they would evenually try to find another way around it. Even though the butte was perilously steep, they just might try to scale it. If they could somehow climb the nearly vertical rock and get above him, the tactics would suddenly shift to their favor. It was something he would have to stay alert to.

Jack waited just to the side of the narrow pass with his cartridges at his side. In a crouch, he rested his left elbow on his left knee, with his right knee on the ground. He could fire with great accuracy from that position, literally hitting anything he wanted. He listened to the small force's movements, still a ways down the trail, with the rifle held loosely in both hands. When the clopping sound of their horses drew closer, he pressed the stock against his shoulder, and lowered the barrel down the slender canyon. Half a minute later, that sound began to echo down the pass.

The first warrior to appear rode with the reins in his left hand and his rifle held in his right. He hadn't seen the man waiting at the end of the narrow passage, or the weapon pointed his way yet, and Jack drew a bead.

Two seconds later, the crack of a single shot announced his presence, as the force of the bullet struck the Apache's long gun at the breech. In that instant of shock and as the Indian's weapon was suddenly knocked from his grip, he came to a momentary stop. Just to make the point very clear, Jack then squeezed off several more rounds in rapid succession. He bounced them off both sides of the rock walls, to either side of the Apache's head, leaving no question that he controlled the situation.

Jack reloaded as the Apache made a temporary retreat. In the lull, he readied for the Indian's next move. He didn't have long to wait. The next attack was what Jack expected. A typical Apache tactic. They sent a riderless horse down the pass as a shield, with a warrior right behind it, spiriting it along with a stick against its flank. A clever ploy, but Jack was ready for it. The pony came in at a fast walk and when it reached the halfway point of the passage, Jack opened fire. Of course he could have simply shot the horse, but he just wanted to stop it. He aimed his rapid fire into the rock wall three feet ahead of the advancing animal. The bullets ripped into the rock at the horse's eye level, causing the hapless beast to be pelted with rock chips and small stones and sprayed with coarse sand all about its eyes. It stopped short, reared briefly, and produced a high-pitched whinny in protest. Jack fired a couple of more rounds to the same effect, and the animal began backing up while shaking its head in annoyed and frightened disapproval.

Again, Jack loaded his rifle and waited. It took a

while, as the determined Apaches tried to overcome their enemy's formidable position. Jack didn't figure there was any chance of them giving up, but he wondered what was taking them so long. Nearly twenty minutes passed and not a sound, not even from above.

Then, with a sudden fury, they opened up with a steady volley of rifle fire. Four Apaches came forward with a clever attack. The two forward men turned sideways so they could both move and fire at once. When they expended their ammo, they'd duck just low enough for the two men behind them to take over firing. The first two would reload during that time. Then, once again, it was their turn to go on the attack. The idea was simple. Keep the enemy pinned down, unable to return fire without exposing themselves to a hail of bullets. How could anyone fire back when the Indians' firing never stopped? Jack stood just around the edge of the slender pass and pondered his options. He had to bring the attack to a halt, but preferred to stop short of killing them.

He waited and listened. The warriors were relentless. They pressed ahead, and were almost halfway through. He then began to notice the rhythm of the firing. It was a nearly steady beat, timed to allow their compatriots to finish reloading and not have lulls in the action. Jack began moving his own rifle slightly back and forth away from his chest, in time with their firing. He turned so his rifle was parallel with the pass, but a few inches from being seen by the advancing Indians. Then, while timing his movement in between the Apache firing intervals, he snapped the rifle out, squeezed off a single round, and then pulled it back to his chest, all in a fraction of a second. After cocking the weapon, he did it again, and again. It wasn't an accurate way of aiming, but he knew it was just a matter of time before he'd hit something. It was in response to the seventh shot that Jack heard the muted moan of a brave Apache taking a bullet. Of course, it wasn't a fatal wound. Jack was careful to direct his shots low. But it broke up the attack. They had to pull their comrade back out of fire and think of something else.

Time ticked by and a firing routine began. The Apaches would fire a round and Jack would answer it. Minutes later it would be repeated. A simple test to see if he was still there. It was also a pretty smart tactic, for Jack was beginning to think that he had given Dan and Fawn a comfortable lead and he wanted to head out too, before any other Apaches arrived. That was a real possibility. The constant exchange of fire could be heard for miles and he knew that those Indians that had split up and headed east earlier, might just hear it and come back to help their brothers in arms. But the minute Jack stopped returning fire, the hostiles on the other side of the narrow pass would know he'd left and then they'd be in hot pursuit. He was stuck.

After another ten minutes of trading bullets, Jack suddenly reeled around, aiming his rifle up trail. The sound of approaching horses coming down the mountain took him by surprise. His attention had been consumed with the action in the pass and the possibility of a hostile finding another way to circumvent it. With his mind and body tensed to expect action from any direction, he barely managed to hold back from firing.

Jack let the rifle drop to his side. He pushed his hat back a little, and shook his head. "What are you doing? You should be miles away by now!" They were still a ways out and he had to shout for them to hear him.

Dan waited until they got closer. "We knew you wouldn't like my little scheme and we didn't want to be talked out of it."

Dan and Fawn brought their ponies to about ten feet from where Jack stood, which was just to the left of the gorge. As they stepped down off their mounts, another bullet came whistling through the slender pass, and Jack replied by stepping over to the edge and squeezing off a single round in the opposite direction.

"What's going on, partner?"

"That's what I want to know." Jack turned back to Dakota.

"I mean, why are they firing one shot at a time?"

"They want to know if I'm still here, but I want to know why you two are here. I thought you'd be halfway down the other side of the mountain, and safe."

Fawn moved close to Jack and put her small hand in his. She smiled up at him. "But we wanted to make sure you were safe too." She looked around to Dan. "Show him, Dakota."

Dan walked, with a decided limp, to the back of

Fawn's saddle, pulled off the saddlebags, and made his way over to Jack. "We brought you a little present. Thought you might have some use for this." He handed Jack the heavy leather bags.

Jack tucked his Winchester under his arm so he could use both hands. After pulling open the flap, a smile spread across his face.

Dan wore a similar expression. "I remembered that my old miner friend had a whole lot of that stuff on hand. He always was kind of a lazy prospector. He'd much rather blast than dig. Anyway, I think that just might even out the odds a mite."

Jack counted twelve sticks of dynamite in each bag. "I think that more than evens things up." He gave them both an approving nod, while closing the flaps back up. Then, after pulling his knife from inside his boot, he cut the wide leather strap that connected the two bags. He handed Dakota one of the bags and then went for his horse. He nudged the big stallion close to the edge of the gorge and tossed the heavy bag about thirty feet in. Then, after cocking the rifle, he glanced back and stated, "You two best move back a ways. This is gonna be loud and dirty."

Fawn helped Dan climb aboard, and quickly swung up into her own saddle. When they got a couple of hundred feet back up the trail, Jack spurred his horse a little ways on up the trail too, before turning to get a clear shot. Jack then fired a single shot into the dynamite-filled bag causing an instantaneous blast that thundered out of the slender canyon in all directions. In the same moment a shock wave cracked the air with a deafening roar and a plume of dust and debris soared up into the sky and out both ends of the pass. The explosion rocked the earth so hard beneath their horses' feet that it caused them to stumble badly, while the concussion of the blast nearly blew Jack out of his saddle. He frantically grabbed the saddle horn in an attempt to stay aboard as debris pelted him like a shotgun filled with rock salt. Small rocks and smaller pebbles along with a storm of sand, hit hard against his right side, causing him to turn away to spare his eyes. He didn't have to use his heels to prompt Chilco away from the oncoming torrent of earth and wind; the big palomino bolted up the trail with Jack holding on. At the same time, Dan and Fawn kicked their mounts into a brief gallop, bringing them to a halt a safe distance up the hillside, where Jack joined them.

The power of the explosion had momentarily ripped open a large hole in the pass, and heaved a cascade of large rocks high into the air. Some large stones, along with a multitude of smaller ones, came down in the area that the three riders had occupied only moments before.

When the dust finally began to clear, they saw that the narrow canyon had collapsed and crumbled rock filled the space that once was a pass. Jack took off his hat and began using it to brush off some of the thick dust that covered his clothes. He smiled at his companions, his white teeth a distinct contrast to the reddish dirt that covered his face. "Well, that ought to hold our Apache friends for a while."

"Hold 'em?" Dakota shook his head. "It likely blew 'em clean off the mountain."

"Well, that wasn't my plan."

"You planned that?" Dan shook his head.

"Yeah. I just overdid it with the dynamite a bit."

"Just a bit, huh? Somehow I thought you knew how to use the stuff, Jack." The corners of Dan's mouth twisted some.

"Well, I guess I do now."

Dan shook his head again as Fawn added, "But you're all right. You didn't get hurt from the blast?"

"A few bruises from the stones, but I'm all right. But we best get back to the village. We need to take care of Dan's leg."

She turned her pony up the trail. "I know someone who can tend to Dan."

Chapter Fourteen

A Case of Honor

The sun was still climbing toward midday when they left behind the crumbled remnants of the pass. Dakota knew the country well enough that he assumed the lead. In spite of his painful leg, he kept up a good pace, spurring his pony up the ascent. With the higher altitude came more trees and even colder temperatures.

Jack had been riding at the back. "How far is it to your miner friend?" Jack was thinking that it was about time to check on his partner's bandage.

"Oh, his claim's none too close to the trail. It'd take us more than a little out of our way. Besides, he's kind of an ornery cuss. I mean, he don't mind seein' me every year or so, but twice in the same day might just set him off."

Jack didn't answer for a few seconds. Of course he

understood Dan's real concern. No matter how he tried to hide it, he was in a lot of pain, and the sooner he got back to the village and got his leg properly tended to the better. But dressings would inevitably loosen from the movement of riding, so Jack called out again. "Hold up a minute, Dan."

After dismounting, Jack passed the reins to Fawn and walked up beside his partner. A crimson-colored blood-stain soaked his pant leg to the knee. Fresh blood was dripping on his boot. The makeshift dressing had shifted. Jack centered the bandage over the wound and firmly retightened it. That stopped the bleeding, but sent an even more intense wave of pain reeling through Dan's leg. Jack looked to his friend. Dakota's eyes were closed to slits and his jaw was tightly clinched. "We've got to stop and fix this dressing often. You've already lost quite a bit of blood, partner."

Dan answered with a single nod. He knew Jack was right and could feel some of his strength slipping away. So, that was how the trip would go, stopping every couple of miles or whenever the bleeding started. All the stopping used up the afternoon. The hours ticked by until the sun finally ducked behind the mountains.

By the time they finally reached the box canyon and the entrance to the hidden city, it was quite cold and dark. Dan was also pretty weak. Once they coaxed their horses through the entrance and rolled the stone door back in place, Fawn quickly went ahead. A minute later, she was descending the first of the two long ladders that led to the cavern village. At the same time Jack and Dan brought the horses through the tunnel-like passage that led to the corral area.

Dan stood and watched as his partner ushered the three ponies into the small fenced pen. But that was as far as Dakota could make it on his own. He grabbed hold of the primitively fastened mesquite railing that made up the corral and used it to let himself down onto the cold stone floor. He leaned back against the railing and heaved a sigh.

Jack quickly took care of the horses, secured the gate, and then walked over to his partner. He sat beside his weary friend, retightened the bandage, and also leaned back against the crude corral. "I'm afraid being my friend comes at a high price, Dakota."

"Well, it ain't always easy, Jack."

"Like right now. We both know that bullet in your leg is because of me. I don't think you bargained for that many Indians coming after us."

"You could say that but I'm not really complainin'. This thing hurts to blazes and I'm feelin' kinda poorly right now, but I've got no regrets."

Jack found himself looking Dan's way and wondering if that could really be true. "You mind telling me why?"

Dan managed a half smile. "Well, it ain't been dull."

"Maybe, but dull doesn't sound too bad right now."

"I think I know what you're drivin' at. Seems like death and trouble are hangin' over us like some kind of cloud. And I'm not so sure that cloud's not still out there waiting for us."

Jack gave a terse shake of the head. "That same feeling been gnawing at me too."

A few minutes later Fawn returned along with three young men. One of them carried a very long rope. It took only moments for them to tie the rope under Dan's arms. They then helped him to the top ladder and started easing him down. The idea was for Dan to climb down the two ladders, but the rope controlled by the three men above him would support most of his weight. Within minutes he was down to the courtyard and received by Chota and the medicine man. After untying the rope, they helped him across the courtyard to his usual quarters. Standing at the entrance to the large bottom-level dwelling was a woman.

By this time Fawn, Jack, and the three young men had also reached the courtyard. After the three men went their separate ways, Jack took notice of the woman by the doorway. She was middle-aged with attractive features. He had undoubtedly seen her before, but had never really noticed her. Of course she wore the customary scant clothing of almost all the women of the tribe. A simple off-white cotton dress cut above the knees with a single strap over the right shoulder. Her raven black hair was short and adorned with turquoise, which was also typical Anasazi fashion. But what struck Jack, as he and Fawn walked closer to her, was her kind face. She seemed to have a very genuine concern for Dan and Jack guessed she was some kind of nurse.

Fawn, who was usually able to sense Jack's curiosity, simply stated, "Her name's Senita. She'll help the medicine man take out the bullet. She's also going to stay and take care of him until he's stronger."

"Mighty nice of her. Is that what she does for the tribe, sort of a nurse?"

"Sometimes. But she helps out the tribe wherever she's needed. You see, she's not married, so she has time to lend a hand to others."

"How come someone so sweet and pretty isn't married?"

"There are more women than men here, so several women aren't married. Too bad, isn't it?"

Jack nodded and glanced inside to check on Dan. They already had him stretched out on a mat and were examining the wound. Dan was obviously in good hands and Jack felt relief about that. He turned back to Fawn, took her by the arm, and headed back a couple of dozen steps to the fountain.

They sat on the edge of the stone and mortar fountain and looked into each others eyes. She took his hand. "This is the first chance I've had to thank you for saving me from LeBoux and his thugs." She smiled in her sweet way, but sensed her man was about to put himself back in harm's way. It took some effort just to make the smile.

"Well, you and Dakota saved my bacon back at that pass. Dynamite has a way of changing the odds. I'd say we're even." Jack returned the smile, but his eyes betrayed him. They seemed distant, like he was trying to work something out.

"Hardly, but what's really on your mind? What are you planning?" She had a pretty good idea, but wasn't about to say it. There was a simple fact; he never was any good at hiding things from her.

"Well, it's not over."

"You're not going back after that bunch of pirates, are you? They'll expect it."

"That's possible."

"Possible? He knows you. He's just waiting for you."

"It doesn't matter. I've got to go back, I'm not a thief. I've got to get the gold back and return it to the Apaches."

"Do you suppose the Apaches might have caught up with LeBoux before they reached Nogales, or have a plan to go in and get their gold?"

"LeBoux and his thugs had a bigger lead on the Indians than we did, and much fresher horses. I don't see how the Apaches could have caught them. And those Indians aren't crazy enough to venture very close to Nogales, not with the Federales stationed there. No, I took the gold and it's up to me to return it."

"I understand; Dan told me where you got it and how you'd want to set things right. But LeBoux has a lot of men, and they'll be on their guard."

"I'll just have to figure something out. But one way or the other, I've got to go back. It's a case of honor."

Although she felt honor was an admirable trait, she never really understood his blind devotion to the code of the West, where strict rules of conduct demanded adherence no matter the cost. "Your sense of honor will get you killed. LeBoux has had the deck stacked against you from the start."

"I think his luck's about to change."

"I'm not so sure, but either way, I'm going with you." There was a determined look in her eyes that left no doubt that she was serious.

Jack shook his head, "No! You can't come. I've got to go alone. I can't protect you."

"Then I'll follow you."

"You'd do it wouldn't you?"

She gave her customary firm nod.

Jack turned his head away, choosing to avoid an argument. He looked across the courtyard, allowing his attention to be briefly distracted by a couple of young boys carrying water back to their home. Then, after a long moment's thought and much to her surprise, he looked her way and returned the nod. "All right, sweetheart, maybe that's not such a bad idea."

Chapter Fifteen

Deception

First light found Jack and Fawn more than halfway to their destination. Jack was betting that LeBoux and his cronies were still in Nogales. It just made sense. He seemed to have some sort of influence there. How else could he have set things up, right down to the man in the jail cell? It also seemed obvious that LeBoux's influence only went as far as the border and there were actually two towns named Nogales, one on each side of the boundary. A mostly technical difference, for most people moved from one to the other without giving the international line a thought. But there was one important distinction between the two, and that was the law. The realm of authority of either town abruptly stopped at the border and as things stood, Jack wasn't welcome south of the boundary. It also seemed pretty clear that LeBoux didn't want to cross north, either.

Jack and Fawn continued to ride south and crossed the cold and rugged desert expanse with few words. It wasn't until the sun finally began bringing some warmth to the morning that she finally asked what had been on his mind for most of the night. She rode up close on his left side and spoke with a slight shiver from the cold. "Are you going to tell me why you gave in so easy?"

"Gave in?"

"Yeah. You were dead set against me coming along one minute and then you suddenly changed your mind."

"Well, I don't like putting you at risk, that's for sure. But I was having trouble working something out. If I'm right, and LeBoux's still in Nogales, I needed to know the lay of the place. I need to know where he and his thugs are holed up and where the doors and windows are. You know what I mean, how to slip in without being seen. What I really need is a spy. So, it occurred to me, after you said you wanted to come, that with your help, we could play a little game of deception."

"What sort of deception?"

"Just a little disguise. I noticed that some of the young boys in the tribe were just about your size. I got to thinking, if we dressed you up like a Mexican boy, you know, with the blousy white pants and shirt and one of those wide brimmed hats they wear, I don't think anyone would pay any attention to you."

A sparkle in her eyes indicated her approval of the notion. "One of the black sashes they wear around the waist would help too. But just what am I supposed to do, ask questions, or just look around?"

"No questions. You're just gonna be the scout. And be careful, don't bring any attention to yourself. But, I figure if you keep that hat low over your eyes you should be able to walk right through town unnoticed. But you'll be able to spot any of LeBoux's boys and where they're at."

"Then I report back to you?"

He nodded.

"And what about you? What's your plan?"

"The same thing. A little deception. It's time to dust off my city slicker clothes. Then, once you tell me the lay of LeBoux's digs, I'll move in and liberate the gold. The city clothes should make it easier to get close without being spotted."

"You make it sound so easy. So why do I have such a bad feeling about this?"

Jack didn't answer, but he also had some doubt eating at him.

Two hours later they passed by the first structures that led into the northern part of Nogales, the American side of the border. They were smallish dwellings of adobe and brick with flat roofs. The homes of the mine workers and their families. A mix of gringo and Mexican laborers worked the mine. This area was mostly

Mexican. Fawn spotted a senora hanging laundry, rode over to her, and told her what she needed. The helpful woman directed Fawn to a nearby house, where she was able to quickly make a deal. The clothes had long since been outgrown by her son and were well worn. Fawn figured that was all the better. The grateful lady was happy to receive two dollars for the tattered garments, and allowed Fawn to change inside her home.

With half the disguises complete, they next headed for a small mercantile at the edge of town. They stepped down from their mounts in front of Miller's Dry Goods and Fawn stayed with the horses. Jack took only enough time to replace the white shirt and gray trousers he'd used for Dan's bandage. He then returned to Fawn on the boardwalk with the shirt and slacks under his left arm. "All right, I don't think we'd better linger here. I'll take the horses down to that livery and I'll wait for you there," he motioned toward the stable at the other end of town. "You make your way over to the Mexican side of town on foot. They might recognize your horse."

She merely nodded. What he said made sense.

"Then just stroll through town and give it a look. Take your time, keep your head down, and act real casual. Maybe even kick a stone and rub your nose once in a while. You know, like a young boy."

She smiled. "Is that what boys do?"

He shrugged. "I don't know, maybe. Just don't let anybody see your face or catch you looking at them."

"I get it."

"Of course you do. I know how smart you are." He started to lean over to give her a kiss.

She abruptly moved back. "I'm a boy, remember?"

He stood up straight and stepped back. "Sorry, that was dumb."

She gave a quick look around to see if anyone was nearby. There wasn't. Then, after giving Jack a single wink, she tilted the crumpled hat down to her eyes and walked away.

As she headed for the pueblo south of the borderline, Jack slid his new duds into a saddlebag and swung up into the saddle. With the reins to Fawn's pony in his left hand, he nudged Chilco up the street. A couple of minutes later he stepped down just before the open barn doors of the unpainted stable. He pulled out all his city clothes from the saddlebag and slid them under his arm. Then he led the two animals into the barn and paid the liveryman for board and feed. While the burly stableman unsaddled and tended to the two mounts, Jack walked into the tack room and quickly changed clothes. He rolled his riding clothes up tight, walked over to where his saddle and gear had been hung and stowed them in his saddlebag. The livery hand glanced Jack's way at that moment. In response Jack touched the brim of his gray bowler and added, "Got a business meeting in town."

The big fellow returned a single nod before getting back to the horses.

It wasn't really a lie. Jack did intend to have a meeting with LeBoux and he definitely meant business. The clothes, he figured, would help him keep that meeting. They were the last piece in his plan of deception. He looked far different in what he called his city slicker clothes. In place of his usual riding duds were the bowler hat, white dress shirt and gray slacks over the boots. But the most important change was the half-length tweed jacket. It not only hid his powerful build, but also his twin Colt .45s. He now simply looked like a business man.

There was nothing left for him to do but wait. He tipped the gray bowler all the way to his eyebrows and walked out and around to the side of the livery. There he stepped back far enough to be out of the line of sight of the townsfolk and leaned against the wall. *As good a spot as any,* he thought.

The time went by agonizingly slow. An hour ticked by and he grew more and more anxious. Every few minutes he'd peer around for a quick look, but there was no sign of her.

He wasn't good at waiting, not when he didn't know if Fawn was safe. And he was the one who had sent her out there, right among LeBoux and his pirates.

Another thirty minutes passed and he started thinking that it must have all gone wrong. He reached down and pulled out each Colt and checked the action and noted that the cylinders had all six rounds. Then he slid the pistols in and out of their holsters. It was a matter of reflex, the drill before battle.

Too much time had gone by. All she had to do was walk through town and do a little looking and it was a very small town. He figured around a half-hour should have done it; now it was three times that long. He made up his mind right then: he could wait no more. It was time to go in and get her and he knew just what that meant. He would saddle up, and figure it out as he went along.

Jack rounded the corner on his way to the livery entrance but stopped short. There she was, just a block away, coming the way they'd come into town. She kept up the ruse. The wide hat tipped forward and she even made the effort to kick a stone as she continued the slow, casual walk. Once he saw that she had spotted him, he made his way back round to the side of the livery and waited.

He lost only some of his anxiety by the time she joined him. Once she got close, she pushed back the hat and gave him a most charming smile, but his expression was still tense, and the words terse. "What happened? What took so darn long? I thought those thugs had you, for sure!"

She moved her head back a little in response as Jack had never spoke to her this way before. But before she had a chance to feel anger, she realized just how scared he had been. That wasn't something Jack was used to. He was man nearly indifferent to danger, with no qualms about putting himself in harm's way and with enough confidence in his own abilities to never display emotion. Yet, she was seeing a different side of him. It was clear that the one thing that could scare Jack was the thought of losing her. She raised her arms, slid her hands around his neck and felt his hands go around her waist. He lifted her gently, and pulled her close for more than a minute.

In that moment, all was forgiven, and nothing needed to be said. Jack's tense expression melted away and by the time he let her down to her feet, there was only a smile. She smiled back in her most charming way and raised her eyebrows a little. "I saw him."

"LeBoux?"

"Yeah, and some of his men. I did just what you said and when I got to the center of town, I spotted his first mate. He was just sitting in front of a hotel called Cuesta Real. So, I just kept walking. I wandered through town but didn't see any others. Then I got an idea." She took her hat off and showed Jack the hole she put in it, just above the brim. "I made a circle and found a place to sit a few buildings away from the hotel. Then I sat down, leaned against a wall, and pretended to be taking a siesta. I put the hat down over my face, but I could see the hotel through the hole. After a while, I saw several more of the captain's thugs. It took almost an hour before I caught a glimpse of LeBoux. He has a room on the second floor. There's a small balcony facing the street. He stepped out, looked around for a few seconds, and went back in."

"What's the hotel like?"

"A typical Spanish building. Adobe, two-story, flat roof. One door in front, and one in back. Windows front and back on both floors, but not on either side."

Jack couldn't hold back a small grin. "You're good at this. Did you notice anything else?"

"Well, I got the impression that they were waiting for something, or someone."

"Could be. Why else would they all be hanging around the hotel?"

"So now what?"

"So maybe I'd better pay LeBoux a visit before that somebody shows up."

Chapter Sixteen

Dropping In

Fawn had waited around the corner of the livery barn while Jack went in and saddled the horses. He also picked up a thirty-foot length of rope from the tack shop and settled the account with the livery man. He knew the rope he already had on his saddle was far too short for what he was planning. After leading both mounts out of the livery and tying them to the nearest hitching rail that ran either side of the entrance, he rejoined Fawn. As he spoke, he tied a loop at one end of the rope he'd just purchased, making it into a lasso. "All right, you wait here until I'm well out of sight. Then head back out of town, the way we came in. I'll meet you back at the village."

She shook her head in her determined way. "No! I'll

wait for you just east of town. If something goes wrong, I've got to be close enough to help."

"If something goes wrong, I want you miles away from this place."

She shook her head again. "I can't help you when you go up against LeBoux and his men, but I'm not leaving you high and dry. I'll wait for you about a half mile east of here."

"No. I have to know you're safe. Now, you've already done your part. This is my play; let me play it."

She seemed to realize it was useless to belabor the point. She finally returned a reluctant nod.

Jack released a noticeable sigh, and wanted to put that little dispute behind. "That hotel, I imagine it's like most Mexican buildings, it has poles protruding just below the roofline?"

"Yeah, they stick out a foot, or more." She smiled warily, easily able to figure out his plan.

"All right then. I shouldn't be too long. You just be careful."

"That's funny, that's what I was going to say." She was doing her best not to show how scared she was, but wasn't too successful. Tears started to well up and she looked away. She wiped away the tears, turned back and gave her best effort at a confident nod. "You just go in there and do what you have to do."

That was Jack's signal to go. And she was right. It was not the time for prolonged displays of affection and good-byes. He needed to clear his mind of everything but the business at hand. They parted with forced smiles and Jack headed east out of town. It only made sense to take the long way around. Once past all the small homes scattered along the outskirts of the business district, he kicked south. After traveling well south of Mexico's Nogales, he began his careful approach into the pueblo. Jack vaguely remembered the Hotel Cuesta Real. A prominent building near the center of town. He turned up the street that ran behind the hotel, stopped, and dismounted. The village was quiet on this backstreet; only a handful of locals could be seen. Jack made sure his coat was covering his guns and his bowler was suitably tilted over the eyes before he began leading his pony up the right side of the street. Six buildings short of the light green hotel, he stopped, tied off the reins to a post, and pulled the rope off the saddle horn.

He moved slowly, staying close to the storefronts, turning occasionally to look behind him. When he reached the hotel, he stopped long enough to glance down the narrow alley that allowed access to the front of the building and the main street of the town. He saw no one and moved quickly to the rear of the hotel.

There was a rear door, but he didn't intend to use it. His plan was to get in and out fast without having to go up against the whole of LeBoux's thugs. After one more look in all directions, Jack took the rope from beneath his coat and spun the lasso a couple times above his head, before tossing it straight up and over one of the protruding poles that supported the building's roof.

Then, after giving the rope one hard tug to secure it snugly around the pole, he used it to pull himself up, hand over hand, until he reached the pole. At that point, he used the pole to pull himself high enough to get his right hand on the edge of the rooftop, then he was able to get his knee over the pole.

He was relatively secure then and peeked over the edge of the roof. No guards, just a flat roof. He pulled and rolled quietly onto the rooftop and began crawling carefully to the front side of the building. In less than a minute, he was flat on his stomach, and looking down on the main street. People were moving freely about in all directions and voices could be heard down in the hotel. There were too many people around to linger where he was, he might be spotted. The upstairs balcony was just below him, less than ten feet to the floor.

Jack noted that the balcony had a decorative iron railing on all three sides. He moved to a point just above the railing before he began to let himself down. He let his feet trail off first, and then, using his powerful arms, eased down until his feet rested on the railing. Using the wall to steady himself, he was able to first bend his knees and then step down silently from the railing to the balcony floor.

Two windows flanked the doorway. From his position beside the nearest window, he took a few seconds to study the interior of the room. A single door stood centered on the opposite wall and two beds rested left and right against each wall. Between them was a small table. LeBoux and his first mate, Billy, sat across from each other at the table playing cards with LeBoux on the left. Saddlebags rested at the foot of the right-hand bed and Jack recognized them as Dan's. It seemed likely that they still contained the gold. Jack figured that was all he needed to know. He pushed the door open, drew both guns and stepped into the two men's quarters. So there wouldn't be any question of who just entered the room, Jack used the barrel of his left pistol to raise the brim of his bowler. "I happened to be in town and thought I'd drop in, boys."

LeBoux and Billy turned his way at the same time, but surprise wasn't particularly evident in either man's eyes. LeBoux, as was his custom, did the talking. "Well, you didn't have to get all dressed up just to pay us a visit, cowboy."

Jack had a very uneasy feeling that he was in a trap, but wasn't about to let the captain read it in his face. He spoke as he moved back toward the window. "I thought you might try to stop me from taking back the gold, so in that case this is the appropriate dress for a funeral."

"Don't think there's going to be a funeral, unless it's yours, cowboy. But you might wish you were dead before long."

Jack heard the footsteps of many men out in the street; voices and commotion could also be heard downstairs in the hotel. He glanced out the window while staying out of the line of fire. Soldiers were forming a line, raising their rifles, and aiming at the balcony door. Jack kept one gun on the two swabs, the other toward the street. "Is this all for me?" He looked straight at LeBoux. "You shouldn't have gone to all this trouble."

"It's no trouble, cowboy. In fact, it's my pleasure."

"Well, it looks like about thirty or forty to one. I guess I'm not gonna live through this anyway, might as well take the two of you first." He aimed both Colts at the two men's heads. "At least this will give me some pleasure." He pulled back both hammers and watched the reaction. Of course Jack had no intention of killing them in cold blood. It was just a ploy. A scare tactic designed to get LeBoux talking. Jack had to know the troops' orders. Were they told to kill or only arrest him? And the only way to coax the captain into revealing that information was to raise the stakes.

"Don't shoot! They're not going to kill you." LeBoux covered his head with his arms.

By this time, many footsteps and the clanking of weapons were rushing up the stairs within the hotel's interior. Jack twisted his mouth and eased the hammers down. "So, it's prison."

LeBoux nodded nervously.

"So, what's the charge?" He slid both pistols back into their holsters, indicating he was resigned to his fate.

The captain exhaled a noticeable sigh and relaxed his defensive position. Jack's yielding gesture was bolstering LeBoux's confidence and Jack could see it in his face. A smug smile spread across the captain's face, where fear had shown only moments before. "Don't worry about that, cowboy. We'll think of something."

Those words were no sooner spoken than far louder ones came from behind the door. "*Señor*! Come out unarmed! Come out now!"

Jack recognized the voice. The same stern-faced corporal as before. And the odds were just as bad as before. There was no card to play. Jack knew it, and so did LeBoux. The captain and his first mate stood up and moved away from the table. They both watched with satisfaction as Jack untied the thin leather straps that secured the holsters to his thigh, unbuckled it from his waist, laid the guns and holster on the table, and stepped to the door. "I'm coming out, unarmed." He slowly opened the door, put his hands above his head, and walked toward the business end of a dozen rifles.

The corporal gave Jack a hard stare before checking to see that he was indeed unarmed. With that done, he left it to his troops to escort the prisoner down the stairs and out into the street. Another twenty or so soldiers waited there and joined in the procession leading back to the jail. It was as before, very businesslike, with no words spoken or chances taken.

Five minutes later, Jack was secured behind bars, the troops had withdrawn, and he was left to ponder his fate.

Chapter Seventeen

LeBoux's Revenge

Hours ticked by in the small, cold, stark cell. It had given Jack ample time to think. LeBoux had been two steps ahead of him the whole time. He had underestimated the captain and found himself in the unusual position of having no plan. In fact, he saw no immediate form of escape. Although the tiny jail cell he found himself in was old, it was a substantial structure, with three-foot thick brick walls and solid iron bars.

Jack reasoned his best chance of escape would be after they removed him from his present residence and before he got to prison. He had heard of a particularly unpleasant prison in Sonora and figured it was his most likely destination. If his guards were a little careless along the way he might just seize the moment and break free. But judging from the number of troops they had used to move him in the past, even that possibility seemed pretty thin.

He had been left alone with his thoughts as the day dragged on and the sun descended toward evening. Placing a guard before the jail was unnecessary. The authorities knew there was no way of escaping those massive walls and bars and they preferred to stay inside the warm police station across the courtyard. But with about an hour before sundown, two men finally entered the courtyard and approached the jail cell. From the smug smile on the captain's face, Jack figured the visit was to relish in the moment. It was also not surprising that Sargento Ramirez accompanied him, for it was obvious that Ramirez was in the captain's employ. Besides, LeBoux had a large ego and probably wanted an audience for his final victory over Jack, that moment of revenge.

For nearly a minute Captain LeBoux stood just a couple of feet from the bars wearing a cocky smirk. Ramirez was right at his side, but he showed only indifference in his expression. This was merely business to him; that seemed plain enough. Jack had the impression that LeBoux wanted him to speak first but he chose not to. In fact, he wanted to get the captain talking, knowing that was his weakness, a tendency to brag and talk too much.

With just a touch of arrogance in the tone, LeBoux finally broke the silence. "I've been waiting a long time for this." He stepped a little closer and gave Jack a confident stare. "Because of you, I lost my ship, crew, and a very valuable cargo, and almost ended up in prison. Now I've got the gold back, you're going to a Mexican prison, and pretty soon I'll have another ship."

"We'll see about that." Jack just wanted him to keep talking.

"No, I've already seen to that. I'm going to enjoy knowing you're living out your days in a miserable prison. Why, I'm going to laugh every time I think about it." He gave a quick chuckle, then regained the stare. "I bet you're wondering just how I got the upper hand on you, cowboy?"

"Not really. It's easy enough to figure." Jack said it with a matter-of-factness that was aimed to irritate him.

"I doubt that."

"Your plan was simple. You paid off officials to set me up, like the sergeant here." He gave a fleeting glance toward Ramirez. "That's how you got your hands on Fawn and forced me to give you the gold. Then, when you thought I might come back, you put out a reward for anyone who spotted me around town, so you and the Army would be ready." Jack said it in dismissive way, hoping to further irritate the captain.

"Not bad, cowboy. That's part of it."

"That's all it is, LeBoux—payoffs, ransom, and bushwhacking."

"You think small."

Jack turned away without speaking, again to rile LeBoux.

"It's also revenge." Anger was starting to tinge the words.

"Try taking that to the bank." Jack glanced back as he moved away from the two men and continued to walk to the rear of the cell.

"When I'm finished, I'll own the bank!"

Jack shook his head, turned and gave a scoff.

"Like I said, you think small. That gold's just the beginning. I'm gonna parlay that into a fortune, and real soon."

Ramirez put his hand on the captain's shoulder and turned him toward him. "You shouldn't be telling him this. Don't tell him any more."

LeBoux shrugged off the hand and scowled, clearly taking exception to his underling giving him warnings. But as they faced each other, Jack noted the appearance of the captain's first mate; once he was halfway across the courtyard, the other two men detected his presence and turned. Billy walked right up to them and spoke quietly.

Jack pretended to have no interest in what was being said. But he was actually acutely listening, straining his ears to catch any part of the message. He only managed to hear two words: lieutenant and daybreak. With so little to go on, he could only guess what his scheme might be. It did seem likely that he was meeting an Army officer at sunup, but even if that was right, it was of little use from in jail.

With whatever information he had received from his

first mate, LeBoux seemed to lose interest in further banter with Jack. He looked one last time into the jail cell and smiled. "Adios, cowboy. Now we're even." They then made their way out of the courtyard with LeBoux and Billy giving a brief laugh at Jack's expense. In less than an hour darkness came and the night grew cold.

Chapter Eighteen

Predictable Nature

By midnight Jack was huddled in a corner, his coat pulled tight, the collar up around his neck. There was little protection from the chill. The bars let the night air swirl around the ten-foot-square cell. The cold stone floor and brick walls penetrated his boots and clothing, the chill cutting to the bone.

Jack was a tough guy and dealt with the cold in his stubborn way, so the temperature wasn't what was on his mind. Of course, just how he'd manage to free himself was of prime concern, but he was also troubled by how LeBoux had read him and played him. Being predictable had gotten him into this and he knew it. Yet it seemed that LeBoux also had his predictable side. His arrogance and pride tended to make him talk too much and even his illegal pursuits seemed to have a pattern.

As Jack put the few pieces he had together, he began to get an idea of what the captain might be up to. It seemed clear that the gold was simply to be used to finance a bigger scheme. The fact that a lieutenant was involved got him thinking about Camp Crittenden. It was less than a day's ride from Nogales and the railroad passed south of the military post and, of course, north of the border. As he thought back to his first run-in with LeBoux, down in Vera Cruz, and the fact that he was a gunrunner, it all began to make sense. Jack would have been willing to bet that just like the captain had done there in Nogales, he had made a deal with someone in the Army. There was probably a shipment of arms unloaded from a west-bound train sometime earlier in the day. But instead of being escorted north to Camp Crittenden by a complement of troops, those soldiers were going to head south to make a deal with LeBoux. And the captain and his thugs were either meeting, or leaving to meet them, at daybreak.

The pieces fit nicely together, for all the good it did. Jack tried to put it all aside, closed his eyes and drifted into an uneasy sleep. A couple of hours later he awoke abruptly. The metallic sound of a key turning in the door lock brought him to his feet.

For just a moment, surprise made him blink. He rushed up to the iron door. "What are you doing here?" He managed to keep the volume down, but there was little question of his disapproval.

"Why, do you like it in there?" The lock opened and she looked up to see Jack's expression soften. Fawn always seemed to know how to take the edge off Jack's anxiety.

"How'd you get those keys?"

"I'll tell you all about it after we get out of here."

That made a lot of sense. Jack responded with a couple of nods, swung the heavy door open and let her lead the way. They quietly made their way out of the courtyard, and she turned left away from the police station and also the hotel where LeBoux and his men were staying, which was another dozen or so buildings beyond the *policia*. As Jack made the turn, he quickly glanced back at the police station. A dim glow filled the small window on the building's side. He saw no one inside. In fact, as he looked up and down the street, he couldn't see a living soul. It was late and the entire village appeared to be asleep.

Fawn continued on for another couple of blocks and at that point, in a particularly dark area of the town, they reached a hitching rail where both of their horses were tied. Jack could easily see that she was feeling the cold. He took the few seconds required to remove his coat, put it over her shoulders, and kiss her.

She hugged him for but a second, and then whispered, "They're in the saddlebag."

Jack reached for his left saddlebag and retrieved his gunbelt. He was also relieved, and slightly surprised, to note that the dynamite still remained. Even his Winchester rifle was still there, resting in the saddle–mounted sheath.

He gave her an approving nod as he strapped his iron around his waist. Seconds later, with the reins around each horse's neck and in each rider's grip, they stepped up into the saddle. Jack looked back at the police station—again he saw no one—and they spurred the ponies smartly up the street and soon out of Nogales.

They rode beyond the last buildings that made up the pueblo and turned north. The horses were kicked to a trot and ten minutes later they had put both townships called Nogales behind them. They were a few miles into the United States and traveling north into the bitterly cold desert. There was a quarter moon above and a still quiet surrounding them. Jack felt that they had put a comfortable distance between their enemies, and the horses were allowed to ease to a slow walk. Fawn brought her mount close to his left side and he turned her way. "So, I'm not complaining, but I thought you agreed to head back to the village."

She made a little shrug. "You were going to take on LeBoux and his men, no matter what. But I couldn't let you go up against them and be worried about me at the same time. So, I misled you a little."

"A little?"

"Well, I had to. You have to admit, LeBoux's been ready for you, able to anticipate your next move. I was afraid he might do it again."

"And he did."

"But he didn't expect me."

"Neither did I. So, how did you get a hold of those keys?"

"I waited until dark, then wandered into town like before, you know, acting like a little boy. I kept my head down and my ears open, and heard them talking about you. They said you were in jail, going to prison, but there hadn't been any shooting. There wasn't much I could do then. I knew I'd have to wait until it was really late to try to get you out."

"So you had a plan."

"Not at first. I found a spot in front of the hotel and pretended to be taking a siesta. I mulled over how to get you out of jail and listened some more. Pretty soon I had a plan and I heard LeBoux's men talking about some big deal."

"They're going to buy guns, right?"

"I got that impression; how did you know?"

"LeBoux likes to talk. I think the meeting's at sunup."

"Probably. I heard them saying something about leaving at four A.M."

"Sounds right. But what about your plan? How'd you get those keys?"

"Well, I had to wait until everyone was off the street to start my plan, which ended up being around midnight, but first I went to a bar and a drug store."

Jack had great curiosity, but let her tell her story.

"I also noticed that your horse was tied in front of the

police station, and I think there was some dispute about who was going to get it. Anyway, I waited until the town was quiet and the police did their shift change at twelve o'clock. Once the new men settled in, I brought them a bottle of mezcal and told them it was from Sargento Ramirez, to help fend off the cold. They accepted that I was just a local boy who ran errands and were extremely happy to get the bottle. Of course, I didn't mention that I poured a whole bottle of sleeping powder in it."

The quarter moon overhead didn't cast a lot of light, but she could clearly see Jack's pearl-white teeth. The grin indicated how much he enjoyed the story.

"I came by a half hour later. Your horse was still tied in front and they were all unconscious. Then it was just a matter of finding the key and your gunbelt—they were both hanging on a wall behind a desk—and putting your horse out of sight. And you know the rest."

"You are such a clever girl. I could say, 'Where would I be without you?' But we both know. In some prison in the Sonoran Desert."

"Well, I'm just glad it's over."

"But it's not."

She seemed to quiver in the saddle, but not just from the cold. She gave him a long stare. "You're not still going after the gold?"

"The gold and the guns. I can't let LeBoux get his hands on those guns. He'll sell them to banditos, Comancheros and every manner of thieves and killers." Jack reached back to his right-hand saddlebag for his other clothes. He pulled his black shirt and vest out and slid them over the white shirt. It wasn't just because of the cold—a white shirt would stand out even on a fairly dark night.

As Jack finished the last of his buttons, she felt compelled to ask, "So, maybe this has to be done, but why does it have to be you? Don't you think it's time to let someone else take care of it? What about the American or Mexican Army, or the U.S. Marshals Office?"

"I don't see how. The U.S. authorites can't cross the border and LeBoux has the Mexican troops in his pocket."

Jack could just see her pretty face well enough to see disapproval and a shake of the head. "Do you have a plan?" Her tone of voice matched her negative gestures.

"I've got some ideas. I wouldn't call it a plan."

"I'm sure you know I'm going along."

"I know. I don't like it, but I'm pretty sure I'm gonna need you. I don't think I'll underestimate you again."

She managed a slight smile. "So, where are we going?"

"East, then south, back into Mexico."

"I was afraid you were going to say that."

Chapter Nineteen

Gunrunners

Not many words were exchanged between Jack and Fawn over the miles that took them east and then south across the border. Jack had much on his mind, not the least of which was keeping Fawn safe while going into harm's way. He hated putting her at risk. Yet he didn't feel like there was much choice. He had to stop the gunrunners and if he'd learned anything, it was that he could count on her. And since she would undoubtedly follow him whether he liked it or not, he might as well have her close enough that they could watch out for each other. Besides, with her clever ideas, he figured there wasn't anyone better to have with him.

As for how he would actually get the guns and gold and not get killed in the process, he was none too sure. At least surprise and darkness were on his side, that along with his two Colts, a Winchester rifle, and the dynamite and fuses.

Fawn finally interrupted his thoughts as Jack turned his pony a little east again. She sided him. "So, how do you know where to find the men selling the guns? Did LeBoux let that slip?"

"I don't actually know where they'll be, but I've got a pretty good guess."

"You're just guessing?"

"You could say that, but I figure LeBoux to be a very cautious hombre. He always has a lot of men around him, pays off the local authorities and even gives a reward for people to be out on the lookout for his enemies, like me. And remember how he led us into that rocky pass so he and his men had the advantage?"

"Yeah, they used the rocks for surprise and cover and anyone aproaching was out in the open."

"Right. I figure he'll use the same spot again, for the same reasons. And if they leave Nogales at four A.M., like you overheard, they could easily get there before dawn."

"So, you think he'll lay for the gunrunners in the rocks. But is that because he doesn't trust them, or do you think he might be planning to double-cross them?"

"I just think he doesn't take chances. He likes to play it safe. So I figure that's where he'll be. It's a protected spot and it worked before."

"So, that's where we're heading?"

"Not yet. I figure the men delivering the guns were given instructions. LeBoux probably told them to go partway and camp for the night. It doesn't figure that he would tell them where he'd be waiting. That wouldn't be playing it safe. Maybe the captain plans to send a man out to bring them in. Who knows? But it doesn't matter if we find them first. I think they're camped somewhere between LeBoux's stronghold and the border. And as cold as it is, they'll have a campfire."

"So, if your right, we'll see the fire."

"Right."

Thirty minutes later they were able to just make out the faint silhouette of Patagonia Mountain against the night sky. They were in the foothills, somewhere between the border and where they expected LeBoux to wait for the guns. If Jack was right, the gunnrunners would be within a few miles, either north or south, of where they were.

There wasn't a lot of vegetation along the gentle but undulating slopes. The brush was sparse, the cactus even fewer and only the occasional mesquite. But the terrain was such that one couldn't see far. It was rolling terrain along this portion of the foothills with large rocks scattered to break up one's line of sight. There was also a small-sized hill just to the north. Jack nudged his mount toward the hill and Fawn came alongside. A few minutes passed and they were at the bottom of the hill. He stepped down from his horse. "I'm gonna clamber on up here and take a look-see." He passed her the reins.

She answered with a nod.

It took several minutes for him to reach the top, having

to negotiate the steeper sections on all fours. Once atop, though, he had enough height to see above the rocks and rising and falling slopes. There was, of course, only the light of a quarter moon but that didn't matter. He was looking for the glow of a campfire, and about a mile to the north he saw one.

He was down the hill, back in the saddle and heading north in only a handful of minutes. A half mile later they rounded a large rock and noted the orange-red glow of the campfire before them.

They rode ahead a little farther and dismounted. Jack knew it wasn't easy for the men to see out into the desert, but he was taking no chances. He needed surprise and wanted to keep Fawn a comfortable distance away. They made a slow cautious approach, then stopped behind a large solitary mesquite, the last cover before getting within the gunrunner's range of vision.

She held both reins as he went to his saddlebags, removed a box of rifle ammunition from the right-side bag and traded the bowler for his Stetson. Then he took about half the dynamite from the other bag. She looked briefly around the mesquite, but couldn't see much more than the wagons barely illuminated by the campfire. "I see four wagons. How many men do you think there are?"

Jack was still finding pockets to hold the dynamite and extra bullets. He spoke without looking up. "Hard to say. There should be at least one man per wagon, plus guards. So, probably eight or ten. Possibly more."

"How can you take on so many?"

"I don't plan on taking on more than one or two. It's got to be what, two, three o'clock? They're gonna be asleep, except maybe one or two standing guard."

"So, how do you do that, you know, take on one or two without them seeing you first and waking the rest of them up?"

"Well, I don't know. But you're right, that's the hard part. I'll have to figure that out when I get closer. Just remember, if things do go wrong, get out of here."

Even in the dim light he saw her eyes narrow and her mouth turn, twisting into a picture of pure defiance. "I'll do what I have to do."

He turned away for just a second. "Well, just don't take any chances." He managed a smile, kissed her briefly but hard, and added, "Hang on tight to these ponies. It's likely to get noisy out there."

Jack moved out in a slight crouch. He had his hat brim low to obscure any shine from the face and made every effort to be silent. As he got closer, he could see from the flickering campfire light that the gunrunners had chosen a campsite up against three very large rock columns that were about twenty feet apart. There was an open space of at least a couple of hundred feet before them. A good defendable position. Beyond that open space, however, were some much smaller rocks. Jack headed that way, staying low until he was almost opposite the gunrunners' position. He moved slower and got even lower, until he finally ended up laying still, flat on his stomach. Still a good thirty feet from the rocks.

There was just one guard. Jack could see him well enough from the campfire glow. He was wearing a blue cavalry uniform. An enlisted man. He was standing in front of the four wagons and seemed to be looking Jack's way. *Did he hear something?* Jack wondered, but the man just stood there. He would just have to wait the soldier out. Minutes passed and in the meantime, Jack looked over the lay of the defenders. The four wagons were lined up before the center rock column. To the left, and in front of an equally large rock, were the troops, bedded down around the campfire. Jack could make out the shapes of seven men under dark blankets. Right of the wagons, some fifty feet away, were their horses, close to thirty of them. They were staked to an area out beyond the three large rocks. Jack noted that there had to be some grass there, since he could tell that the horses were grazing.

After what seemed a very long five munutes, the guard was on the move again and started to head toward the campfire. Within seconds, Jack crawled to the first of the smallish rocks he planned to use for cover. Quickly he went, one by one, until he was nearly across from the horses. It had been his intention to cross the open field even farther behind the horses, so he'd be out of the guard's range of vision, and then slip in the camp from behind. But the guard was at that moment kneeling over the fire, and pouring a cup of coffee. Jack could see that clearly from the firelight. In that second, it also occurred to Jack that the guard would temporarily lose his night vision from his proximity to the flames.

Jack decided to go from where he was. He had over two hundred feet of open ground to reach the horses. The only cover in between were the occasional sage bushes. There weren't many of them and they were small. He would have to move fast and figured he would need the use of both hands. He left his rifle beside the rock and headed across the open field, hoping the crackling fire would cover his sounds. But as he approached the grazing horses, one spooked, which sent a nervous reaction through the herd. The animals moved with a startled jump, and were soon pulling on their tethers and doing a bit of snorting.

The frightened horses would likely alert the guard, there was little question of that, but Jack had already made his move. In an effort to quiet the startled mounts, he darted left, away from them, and made a run for the wagons. He only managed five steps before he heard the clink of a metal coffee cup being dropped. Jack hit the dirt too. He moved ahead on his knees and forearms, with the cover of the wagons still some sixty-odd feet away. Seconds later, he heard footsteps. The guard was making his way around the wagons. Jack became still, but then noted a small sage a few yards to his left and began rolling quietly that way until he was behind it. He laid there, flat on his stomach, looking by the base of the little bush.

A moment after, he saw the trooper slowly coming his way. The man held a Winchester chest high, at the ready. Jack began to slowly move his right hand to his side until he felt the pistol's grip firmly in his hand. He tensed as the man closed the distance, step by step. With only a couple of dozen steps between them, the soldier started to lower the barrel of his rifle and Jack braced for action.

It was the last thing that Jack wanted. Once he fired, it would only be a matter of seconds before the rest of the troops took up the fight. But a fight seemed inevitable. Then, as the soldier began to turn the rifle toward Jack's position and Jack put his thumb atop the hammer of his Colt, the horses jumped again. It was obvious to Jack that it was the trooper's movements that startled the already skittish animals, but the soldier turned and headed their way. Jack quietly sighed, eased the grip on his pistol and watched him walk into the dimmer light, carefully following the man's movements until he disappeared behind the nervous horses. Jack then made his move. It was his chance and there would likely be no other. With careful actions, trying not to make a sound, he headed for the wagons.

The four wagons were side by side, standing parallel to the great rock behind them. Within seconds he found his way to a place of adequate cover, ducking under the second wagon and blending with the shadows. There he waited, crouched low with a Colt .45 in his right hand.

Jack had to take care of the guard. Yet the man was quite alert, his senses heightened from the spooked horses. Moments passed and then the sound of footsteps caused Jack to peer between the large rear wheels and see the trooper coming around the horses again. It seemed that the man had relaxed some. He held his rifle along his side with only his right hand as he walked slowly back toward the wagons. Without stopping, he gave another glance behind him and then started turning, as though he intended to go around the wagons. As the soldier turned in that direction, Jack quietly and very slowly started making his way to the back of his covering wagon.

The guard looked to be heading back to the campfire. Jack reasoned this would be his best chance to take him, perhaps the only one. As the soldier rounded the outermost wagon, he'd make a slight turn. That's when Jack would make his move. Moments passed, and as the trooper reached that point, Jack rolled out from just behind his wagon and quietly got to his feet. That maneuver took only seconds, but the trooper was already a good three steps in front of him.

The plan was simple: come up from behind and knock him out. The butt of his Colt was a suitable instrument, however he had to be very close to use it. Jack took his first step to close the distance, but as soon as his foot struck the ground, the soldier stopped and spun his head around. Jack still had some momentum and came forward in a rush. At the same time, the trooper pivoted right on his heels while reeling the Winchester around. Jack still held his pistol in his right hand but didn't want to use it. Instead, as he lunged forward and the distance between the two men closed to but a couple of feet, he used his forearm to deflect the barrel of the rifle. And then, nearly instantaneously, he followed that blocking maneuver with a hard left punch to the man's jaw. The trooper's legs immediately went out from beneath him, causing Jack to grab his arm and rifle before they both hit the ground with a loud thud.

Jack had been fast but also lucky. He had been fast enough to end the fight before the man had a chance to call out or fire his weapon. But it was mighty close. After letting the soldier quietly down to the cold earth, he looked over to the remaining troops by the fire. All were still.

With no time to waste, he first went for the horses and cut their tethering ropes. Then he came back to one of the wagons and pulled up a section of the dark green tarp between the securing ropes. With the contents revealed, he took a quick visual inventory. At the back of the wagon were boxes of rifles; at the front were boxes of ammunition and several barrels of gunpowder. Working quickly, he affixed four sticks of dynamite with a three-foot-long fuse. He went to each wagon and placed a single explosive device between the barrels of black powder and the ammo. Then, as quickly as he could, he lit each fuse in the wagons.

Although the time was short before the fuses burned down to the dynamite, he wanted to avoid more killing. He knelt down and lifted the unconscious trooper over his shoulder before hurrying across the open space back to the rocks where he had left his Winchester. With only seconds left, he dropped the soldier, grabbed the rifle and began pouring rapid fire all around the sleeping soldiers. The horses scattered. The troops, in their startled condition had no choice but to run for cover and that cover was the great rock behind them. That was, of course, Jack's intention, for they would surely all be blown to bits if they stayed where they were.

The seven men scrambled behind the rock, and no sooner had they done so, the first of four detonations rocked the still night. In a matter of seconds, the four explosions sent a flash of light high into the sky, the blasts disintegrating the wagons and their contents. Debris, heavy dust, and all manner of rock blasted everything in its path. The ground shuddered, while the concussive force deafened the ears and senses.

Jack had managed to pull the soldier and himself behind the rock with the first blast. As soon as the pelting projectiles stopped and while the thick, choking dust cloud smothered the already dark night, Jack began making his way back to Fawn.

Chapter Twenty

Stronghold

Jack managed to keep some semblance of direction as he negotiated his way back to Fawn through the thick dust. As he got closer, it became a little thinner, finally making it possible for him to spot the solitary mesquite that she and the horses were hiding behind. She heard his approaching footsteps and met him with the barrel of one the pistols from his saddlebag pointing right at his head. With reins tight in her left hand and the revolver in the other she stepped closer and stared at the figure before her, but even through the dust and dark of night she recognized him. He wore a heavy layer of dirt that masked his features with only the gleam of his eyes revealed. But that was enough. She felt her anxiety slip away and let the weapon hang by her side. Then, with her free hand, she took hold of his shirt and pulled him close. After taking just long enough to wipe the dirt from his mouth, Jack lifted her until their eyes and then their lips met.

He set her down easy while announcing, "Well, the guns are blasted to kingdom come."

Fawn passed him the weapon and he went to return it to the saddlebag as she spoke. "Do we really have to go after LeBoux since the guns are destroyed?"

He slid the pistol in the saddlebag and turned back to her. "As long as he has the gold, he'll find more guns and sell them to the wrong people."

"But won't he know something's wrong? Wouldn't he have heard the blast or even seen the flash?"

"I wouldn't worry about that. We're quite a ways from Nogales and there are mines on both sides of the border. They all use dynamite. The sound of explosions is common around these parts." He took his reins from her and climbed aboard his mount. "I think we've got the advantage this time."

She also swung up into the saddle, but from her expression and silence there was little question that she didn't share his confidence.

Thirty-odd minutes later they were approaching the labyrinth of large rocks where LeBoux and his cronies had bushwacked Jack and company and kidnapped Fawn. As they neared the rocky pass that had come to be LeBoux's stonghold, Jack studied the lay of the terrain and began to form a plan. What had been a wide trail through fairly open country, dotted with a scattering of varied-sized rocks, funneled down to a passage between two hillsides and a web of great rocks. The only way through it was to wind in and around the towering stones.

Jack had to first figure where the captain would position his thugs. He remembered how LeBoux had let him and his two companions ride far enough into the pass that his men were able to surround them before springing the trap. But he couldn't do that this time; the wagons were simply too big to go between the rocks. *No, he'd have his men waiting behind the very first rocks where the wide trail ended.* He looked left for a suitable place for Fawn and the horses to hide. There, a good hundred feet away, and close to where the hillside rose steeply up, stood the last rock sufficiently large to conceal them.

Jack stepped down from his pony and pointed through the dim light toward that rock. "You go ahead and find cover behind that last rock. I've got a little work to do here."

She gave a nod, turned that way, and Jack went to his saddlebag. After retrieving three sticks of dynamite and a length of fuse from the bag, he went to the closest of the three great rocks that met the trail and pulled out his knife. Right at the base of the rock, he knelt and used his knife to bore a hole straight down. He made it several inches deep, inserted a single stick of dynamite into the hole, leaving about three inches of the explosive protruding above the ground. He then inserted five-second fuses into the other two sticks and slid them behind his belt as he walked over to rejoin Fawn.

She had found a substantial sage surrounded by some grass and had the two mounts tied to the bush so they could do a little grazing. Her arms were crossed, attempting to hold in a little warmth and she was shivering slightly. Jack held her for a minute before she said a word.

"What happens now?"

"We wait. They should be here pretty soon."

"And when they come?"

"I'll get the gold, one way or another."

"How?"

"First I'll ask him for it. If that doesn't work, I'll take it from him."

"Just like that."

"It'll get loud, and it could get bloody, but I'm taking the gold."

The first faint glow announcing sunup appeared behind them above the mountain. The new light allowed the tension in her pretty face to be clearly seen. "I don't have a good feeling about this. I hope LeBoux doesn't show. He seems to anticipate your plans."

Jack turned back toward the rocks, hearing sounds in the distance that could only be horses' hooves. He looked back to Fawn. "It seems we both can predict each other's plan. They're coming in from the other side of the pass. At least I got that right." He managed a little smile. "I've got to get closer. You stay here. Hang on to the horses. We may have to get out fast." He gave her a fleeting kiss and moved ahead to a much smaller rock residing about half the distance to the three large rocks where he planted the charge.

With the arrival of morning twilight, visibility was improving. Pretty soon the light spread across the landscape although in a muted tone, as the sun had not yet come into view. Jack pulled both Colts from his holsters, checked that they were loaded and the action worked properly. As he slid them back, the sounds of at least ten men and horses stirred the area behind the great gray rocks. Voices joined the other noises and Jack could tell that they were dismounting.

Without showing much of himself, Jack took a peek around his covering rock. Two men were standing between the tall rocks where the trail entered the pass. Just where Jack figured. That was of some relief—still there were a lot of men to deal with. Less than a minute later several more were standing there, looking down the trail. It seemed clear that they were expecting company and were more than a little impatient about it. Jack recognized a couple of them. Billy, the first mate and the man he'd seen at the cafe in Tucson, right down to the bowler. Another minute ticked by and the man himself made an appearance. LeBoux stood among his men, also staring on down the trail.

Jack decided to make his presence known. He shouted in the captain's direction. "LeBoux! We've got some unfinished business!"

All the men between the rocks dashed back for cover and grabbed their guns. After a few moments' delay and with surprise and a good deal of agitation in the tone, LeBoux returned, "You've got an annoying habit of escaping and surviving, cowboy. How'd you get out of that jail cell?"

"Your friends put people into jail; mine get them out."

"And how'd you know I'd be here?"

"You've got your spies; I've got mine."

"So, what do you want?" The agitation in his voice was growing.

"Just give me the gold and I'll let you go."

"Let me go? Really? Well, it just so happens that I've got twelve men in here."

"And it just so happens that I've got twelve bullets in my two guns."

LeBoux was clearly tiring of the banter. "And there's another eight men on their way."

"I'm afraid not, LeBoux. I met your friends earlier this morning. They won't be coming."

"I don't believe you."

"Yeah, I think you do. And I think we've talked enough."

"Then come in and get your gold, cowboy."

"Suit yourself. You know what they say, action speaks louder than words. Sometimes much louder." Jack took careful aim at the stick of dynamite. It was a small target, only a few inches of it visible above the ground. He squeezed the trigger, causing an instantaneous explosion that blasted dirt and stones violently into the air. As Jack had figured, having the dynamite drilled down into the ground created a crater at the base of the big rock and a great deal of dirt and dust pluming up into the air.

That was just the first step, which was needed to cloud the enemies' range of vision so Jack could make his move. He found his way to the great rocks, very close to where the blast had just occurred. Knowing that the men within the rocks had to move back in response to the explosion, he began step two. After taking a box of matches from his vest pocket, he put the wooden end of two of the matches between his teeth, clasped a .45 in his left hand and started moving in. He didn't have much time. The dust cloud would soon begin to clear and so would the clouded minds of LeBoux's men.

Jack was pretty sure of where the gold would be. He had seen the captain and he wasn't carrying it. That meant it was still on his horse. And knowing what a cautious hombre he was, he figured the horses would be back some, in case there was trouble, and there would be a man tending them. Once he was a few steps within the rocky pass he heard the animals making nervous snorts and whinnies, their hooves striking the ground. Jack moved faster, in spite of the poor visibility. He used his ears for direction and his right hand to defend against contact with the great rocks. The dust grew a little thinner and he could make out a dozen or so mounts and a single man trying to calm them down. He had his back to Jack and the tether line in both hands. He was pulling back hard to control the rearing horses. There would be no better opportunity. Jack rushed the man, but just as he got within a step of him, the man turned his way. Without hesitation, Jack threw a single right punch, his fist hitting square against the side of the man's face. He went down hard and would be out for a while.

With the dust in the air beginning to thin, Jack moved fast. He grabbed the horses' tether line to quell the bolting animals. Four horses to his right was LeBoux's pony and he quickly worked his way over to it. Once he pulled the two ties securing the saddlebag, he lifted the heavy leather bags onto his left shoulder. No sooner had he done so, he began to hear rustling sounds all around him. The captain's men were on the move, gathering themselves after the initial shock of the blast and apparently getting back in the fight.

Jack stuck to his plan. He took the precious seconds required to take his knife from his boot and cut loose LeBoux's string of horses. As soon as that was accomplished, he pulled a match from his mouth, struck it against the bottom of his boot and lit both sticks of dynamite. With his customary speed, he tossed one stick left and one right, then he hit the gound and covered his head. They landed some thirty feet out in both directions. His intention was as before. Not to kill, but rather to daze his foes and put enough dust in the air to cover his exit. In fact, just the sound and sparkling display of the burning fuses caused the few men close to where the dynamite landed to run for it.

The two explosives blew almost simultaneously. Sand, rock and a concussive blast ripped through the great rocks. A deafening roar punished the ears and stunned the senses. While the last of the pelting stones still battered his arms and sides, Jack got to his feet and headed back out of the rocks, trying to retrace his previous route. The air was a wall of dust, requiring him to grope and stumble his way along, while putting his hands ahead in defense of what might be in his path. Still, he knew his sense of direction was reasonably good and drove on with almost reckless speed. Once he managed to find his way past the two great rocks, where he had planted the earlier charge, he dashed to the right. The dust was thinner there. The many rocks between there and the source of the explosion contained some of the dense cloud. He hadn't counted on that. He was out in the open and what dust there was wouldn't conceal him. With only about a hundred feet to reach Fawn and the horses, he ran for it.

Encumbered by the gold-laden saddlebags, he was doing his best to make speed. Then, as he got to full stride, he felt a sharp sting in his right thigh and heard the crack of rifle fire in the same instant. The leg gave way and Jack was down. He rolled half a turn before looking back at the man who had just shot him. The man was but forty feet away, had just finished cocking his Winchester and was pulling the stock against his shoulder to take aim. There was no time to think and barely enough time to get off a single shot. Both men went for the kill. Jack drew his Colt while his enemy squeezed the trigger of his rifle. Two shots rang out with one loud bang! You couldn't distinguish one from the other. A long crack of fire ended the duel as quickly as it had begun. One bullet headed straight for Jack. The man with the Winchester had gone for a chest shot and his aim was dead center. The other bullet was a head shot, hitting the rifleman right between the eyes. Those cruel eyes, just below the bowler. Jack had sensed that the man would be trouble.

LeBoux's man lay dead, killed instantly. Jack was motionless, flat on his back and having trouble getting his breath. His chest felt like it had been struck by a sledgehammer, a deep, penetrating pain spreading across to his rib cage. Instinctively, he raised his head to see the wound. He had received the full force of a rifle bullet fired at close range. His eyes narrowed when he saw where the heavy slug had hit. The bullet had struck the saddlebag that draped over his shoulder, the gold nuggets within stopping it and saving his life. Jack briefly pondered luck and fate, noting that two inches lower and the bullet would've missed the saddlebag and he'd also be dead.

But the battle wasn't over. Jack saw another of LeBoux's men through the swirling dust cloud in among the rocks. He fired a couple of shots that way to hold him off. It wouldn't be long before the whole of them joined the fight, and Jack was having trouble getting to his feet. Then, just as he managed to stand, two shots were fired from within the rocks and Jack couldn't even tell where they came from. Both rounds whistled by his head and he was more than a little concerned. But then, from his left, he heard another sound. Hurried footsteps came rushing in and then a nearly silent projectile flew by, landing over in the rocks, toward LeBoux's men.

The soaring object was a stick of dynamite, thrown by Fawn, and as soon as it struck the ground, Jack put a slug into it. The blast knocked Jack right back onto the ground with a dull thud and he winced with pain. It also turned the battle for the moment. Fawn was at Jack's side in seconds and had him back to his feet. A half minute later she was helping him up onto Chilco. She swung quickly into her saddle and they spurred their horses to a full gallop.

Chapter Twenty-one

The Honor Code

Three miles passed beneath their horses' hooves before they brought them to a stop. Jack's right pant leg and boot were soaked with blood; his wound would have to be tended to. They were out in fairly level terrain, with only brush and smaller rocks surrounding them. It was a good place to apply a dressing to his bleeding thigh, for they could see trouble coming from quite a distance.

That possibility was slight. All the explosions back in the rocks would have certainly driven off the horses in LeBoux's stronghold. Jack liked the idea of the captain and his band of pirates walking back to Nogales. And with LeBoux suddenly without funds, he just might find himself in a tight spot. His men would still expect to get paid, and very likely the Mexican authorities he made deals with would as well. At least there might be some justice in that.

Jack stepped down from his mount and sat on the cold sandy ground. Fawn did the same, sitting alongside the wounded upper leg, but facing Jack. She gently tore the pant material, both up and down, and inspected the bloodied gash. It was not unlike Dan's wound, the bullet lodged deep in the fleshy part of the thigh, but missing the bone. Other than affixing a dressing to stop the bleeding, there was nothing that could be done out on the trail. It was quickly decided that Jack would sacrifice another white shirt to make the bandage. He would feel the cold a little more without the inner white shirt, but the dressing was more important.

Fawn had been strangely quiet, even while she tended his leg. It wasn't until they saddled up and traveled another couple of miles that she finally broke the silence. "You don't still intend to deliver this gold back to the Apaches?"

Jack was feeling slightly woozy and his leg was paining too, but he tried to sound as though he was unaffected by it all. "Yeah, I know you think I'm crazy, but I won't feel right about it until I return that gold."

"Think about what you're saying. You can hardly walk. What happens if something goes wrong?"

"Why would you say that, when everything's gone so smoothly up until now?" He managed a brief smile.

"I'm serious! This is no time to take on a band of

angry Apaches." The tone was uncharacteristically sharp.

"Well, I don't plan on taking them on. I just want to drop it off at their doorstep, so to speak."

"You're right. I think you're crazy." She would never understand this reckless adherence to his honor code. Yet she knew it was as much a part of him as his love for her. He would go into the Apache canyon because he felt it was the right thing to do, in spite of the risk, or the fact that he was in no condition for a fight. And a fight was the last thing he wanted. He had no quarrel with the Apaches. Still, though she would say no more about it, she didn't like it one bit.

It wasn't long before they were riding along the red cliffs that hid the entrance to the secret canyon so well. Jack kept a sharp eye for dust in all directions that would indicate hostiles returning to the Devil's Canyon. Seeing none, he went ahead with his simple plan. He would leave Fawn with the horses hiding in the wash, as before, and then go into the canyon on foot and leave the gold where they could see it. Leaving his horse behind was a measure of caution. He could be silent and relatively unseen without the big stallion.

Five minutes, Jack figured, that's all the time it should take and they'd be on their way. After a kiss and a look of disapproval from Fawn, he began making his way to the slender passage concealed in the red cliffs. The weight of the saddlebags and his painful leg slowed his progress, but he was soon making his way down the passage.

Once he reached the end of the passageway, he peered carefully into the canyon. More than a dozen warriors were gathered outside the corral by the huts. About half were already mounted; the rest were in the process of getting on board. Jack's timing was obviously bad. Those riders would be heading his way, that was certain. He dropped the gold-filled saddlebags right where he stood and made the best speed possible back out of the passage entrance. But then, just as he reached the end of the narrow shaft, he heard the sound of horses ahead, from out in the desert. He gave a quick glance around the edge of the opening and saw two Apache riders heading right for the canyon entrance at a trot. They were no more than a couple of hundred yards out.

He could take them out and then make for the horses, but that would only lead the Apaches coming from the canyon to Fawn. He'd also had enough of killing; he wasn't there for that. Jack stepped back and tried to think of options. Perhaps it was from the blood loss, but his mind and senses were dulled and Jack did something quite out of character. He hesitated. In those moments of indecision, the possibility of options disappeared, and he heard the Apaches approaching from both sides of the slender corridor.

They couldn't rush him; the passage was too tight for more than one or two riders to come at him at a time. *Yeah, I just might be able to take the lot.* But he was there because of a sense of honor, and he saw nothing honorable about killing men that were only defending their own people. Fawn had been afraid that his code of honor would get him killed. Jack was now thinking the same thing, as he dropped his gunbelt and put his fate in the hands of the Apache.

Jack waited near the center of the passageway. Only seconds passed before the two riders coming into the canyon from the desert stopped abruptly and pointed their rifles at him point-blank. Surprise and then anger were displayed on the two warriors' faces as they studied their quarry. Jack also took note of his captors. They were young men, with hard, lean statures and raven-black hair to their shoulders. They were clad in crudely stitched deerskin; their only weapons were rifles. After what seemed a long moment of sizing each other up, the lead rider motioned Jack ahead. Their prisoner complied, walking, as best he could, toward the canyon.

The sounds of the two horses coming through the passage had alerted the other Apache riders who had intended to leave the canyon. They were all waiting, just outside the passage, and seemed taken aback and more than a little annoyed to see the prisoner. More rifles were quickly pointed Jack's way, and as he stepped a few yards into the canyon, one of the riders from behind rode up close to him. Then, suddenly, things went black.

Jack lay face down on the canyon floor with a trail of blood running by his ear and down the side of his face. The butt of a rifle had struck the back of his head hard enough to knock the average man out for hours.

One hour had passed but Jack couldn't know that. He

lifted his head slowly and opened his eyes. His senses and vision were badly blurred; his head throbbed with pounding waves of pain. It took a little time before his mind began to come around. He didn't know how long he'd been out, but from the way his head felt, he figured quite a while.

He began to remember things like what happened and where he was. That didn't make him feel any better. He looked around at the strange place where he found himself. That didn't make him feel any better either. He was in an area of the Apache mine. Torches flickered a dull glow that allowed him to see a dark pit before him, much like the glory hole where he had commandeered the gold, but smaller. A single pole lay across the open pit. The ends of the pole rested in recesses in the walkway that surrounded the abyss, to keep it in place. A rope was looped around the center of the pole. One end of the rope was coiled up to Jack's left. The other end was by his feet.

On the opposite side of the pit were large golden statues. They were made in the same primitive way as the ones he had seen earlier, but these were different. They were warriors, but with faces of death. Skulls for heads and skeleton for bodies. Above the skeletal warriors was a single golden reptilian creature. Adorned with horns upon its menacing head and a forked tail, it seemed the creature represented the devil. It was plain that Jack was in a place of death.

A young Apache was nearby to Jack's left, and when

he saw that their prisoner had come to, he went to tell the others. Jack had little choice but to await his fate. He was trussed up like a hog, his hands, arms, legs and feet tightly bound with heavy rope.

As Jack's eyes followed the young man's exit, he realized where he was. The great pit where he'd watched the metalworker and taken the gold was just to his right. The dark passage he'd hidden in was the entrance to this chamber of death. Without torch light, he just couldn't see it.

Six men entered the dome-shaped chamber. Jack was struck by the tall man that stayed back in the tunnel-like entrance. He, unlike the other five, was resplendent in gold. Bands of the precious metal encircled his waist and arms. Golden chains hung heavy around his neck, while bracelets, anklets and rings surrounded his limbs. Atop his head was what could only be described as a feathered golden crown. *Some sort of chief*, Jack figured.

Of the other five, four stayed back, while one approached Jack and kneeled beside him. Wearing the usual deerskin and a solemn expression, he spoke with surprisingly good English. "Tell me who you told of this place."

Jack looked him straight in his cold dark eyes. "Your secret's safe. No one will come here. No one will come after your gold."

That wasn't the answer the man wanted. He asked again, but louder. "Who did you tell of this place and where are they?"

"I don't want your gold and no one will come here again. That's all I can tell you."

With that response, the grim-faced Apache motioned to the four men behind him. In seconds, they had tied an end of the rope to Jack's feet and started sliding him to the edge of the abyss. Then three of the men went to the coiled end of the rope, while the one that stayed with Jack, pushed him over the edge.

Jack fell a dozen feet before the slack ran out and his weight hit hard against the rope. A sudden jolt brought his descent to a stop and, momentarily, he swung from side to side. Then the men up top started lowering the rope.

Jack wasn't prone to claustrophobia, but being bound with ropes and lowered into a dark pit of the unknown would bring it to anyone. He found himself desperately fighting against the ropes in a near panic state. Then as the futility of his efforts sunk in, he gathered all the concentration he could muster, and tried to control his fears and save his energy. Just as his breath and heart started to slow a little, he sensed a most unpleasant smell. *Rotten eggs,* he thought and then realized what was below him. Sulfur dioxide. A heavy gas that comes from volcanic action and is deadly poisonous. It was also an extreme irritant and was already starting to burn his eyes and skin. Jack was still going deeper into the toxic gas and he had but one defense, to hold his breath for as long as possible.

A minute passed by and Jack was nearly unconscious.

His mind blurred and his lungs felt like they could burst. Then, he felt the rope start pulling him up again. Seconds later he could wait no longer. He exhaled and took in the noxious fumes, again and again. His lungs burned, but the concentration of gas was less as he rose higher in the pit. Soon the air was good again.

Once he reached the top, he was pulled onto the flat walkway that surrounded the lethal pit. The grim-faced warrior went to him and kneeled beside him. "Who knows of this place and where are they?"

"I told you, no one wants your gold. Why do you think I brought it back? But I don't expect you'll believe anything I say." Jack breathed heavily and braced for another bout with the gas.

The interrogator rose to his feet, and once again motioned to the other men, but Jack noted that the chief was no longer present. He was then pushed over the edge and the routine was played out again.

The second time nearly finished Jack. As they pulled him higher, he was in and out of consciousness, his mind and vision going from reality to a murky mist. He was seeing stars among dark shadows. He was close to death, with only his stubborn will clinging to life.

As he was pulled again up onto the walkway and onto his back, Jack let out a long sigh and looked up in fleeting coherency to see his captor's grim face, but it wasn't him. Jack lowered his eyebrows as though questioning his eyes and mind. He blinked and looked again. "Chota?"

Chapter Twenty-two

Lady Luck

Jack and Dan stood atop the ceremonial Kiva and looked across the courtyard as the brides-to-be reached the steps. How beautiful they were. Each wore cactus flowers in their hair and turquoise jewelry around their waist, necks and wrists. As they slowly climbed the stone stairway, Dan gave his partner a nudge to the ribs with his elbow. "How'd we get so lucky, Jack?"

"Lucky. That's the word, Dan." Jack thought about how he'd been on the both sides of Lady Luck recently. Mostly bad luck during his dealings with LeBoux. But lucky to have friends like Dan, Chota and Chief Tecanay. And very lucky, indeed, to have Fawn.

It had been over a month since Chota rescued him from the Apaches. It was three weeks ago that he told Jack the story. He first explained how the Anasazi had made peace with the Apache in the canyon years ago. It came about when they found a wounded Apache boy in the desert, brought him back to the village and saved his life, much like they had done for the conquistador. But later the boy escaped and made his way back to the canyon. The Apache chief was a grateful and wise man. He sent the boy back with the promise that the Apache would keep their secret. Since then, the two tribes would renew their pledge of friendship every seventh spring. So, when Dan felt up to telling Chota how he caught the bullet, and that Jack was planning on paying the Canyon of Gold another visit, Chota headed that way. By the time he'd gotten there, he found Fawn outside the canyon, about to do something desperate. Chota then went inside the canyon alone and was allowed to meet with the Apache chief. Of course it required some negotiation and assurances, but he managed to secure Jack's freedom. Just what those assurances might be, Chota didn't say.

Jack was lucky to have even survived his day with the Apaches and he knew it. And now was another lucky day. Dan and Senita had fallen in love, as nurse and patient sometimes do. Jack had been in love with Fawn for some time, but it took a succession of close calls, and a brush with the Apache's chamber of death before he finally realized what was important. He also had had more than enough of killing. Dan had been right. A reputation comes with a high price. Too high. He found that out the hard way.

He could be happy there in the Anasazi city, he was

sure of it. There was too much blood and death waiting for him in the world above. This was where he belonged, with Fawn at his side.

Villagers were assembling in the courtyard. Wellwishers and friends. Chief Tecanay would be the last to join the wedding party. He would say the vows and Chota would translate. As the two couples gathered on the great altar, Chota came up to Jack and shook his hand, adding, "I need tell you something, Jack. Now that you're strong again."

"What's on your mind, Chota?"

"I not tell you something about Apache because you were so weak then. I had to make promise to their chief before he let you go."

"What sort of promise?"

"That you help them like you help us."

"The bank?" Jack's eyes narrowed, and he glanced at Fawn.

Chota nodded. "Yes. You take their gold to bank for them."

Fawn gave her fiancé a blank stare. "That's where the trouble usually starts."